Naughty KING

A SEXY MANHATTAN FAIRYTALE: PART ONE

Michelle A. Valentine

Contents

Naughty King
Books by Michelle A. Valentine

Chapter I: The Curse
Chapter II: Dirty Laundry
Chapter III: Tension
Chapter IV: Unexpected Complication
Chapter V: Countdown
Chapter VI: Brother Knows Best
Chapter VII: No Escape
Chapter VIII: Provocateur
Chapter IX: Falling
Chapter X: Mr. Yamada
Chapter XI: Round Two
Chapter XII: Holy Shit

About the Author

The Naughty King
Published By: Michelle A. Valentine Books, LLC

Cover Art by:
Romantic Book Affairs Designs
(stock photos purchased)
www.rbadesigns.blogspot.com
Edited by:
Editing for Indies
www.editing4indies.com
Interior Design and Formatting by:
Christine Borgford, Perfectly Publishable
www.perfectlypublishable.com

For questions or comments about this book, please contact the author at michellevalentineauthor@gmail.com

Sign up for Michelle's Newsletter (https://www.facebook.com/AuthorMichelleAValentine/app_100265896690345)for Exclusive Giveaways & theMost Up-To-Date Info on New Book Releases!

Disclaimer: This book is intended for adult audiences due to strong language and naughty sexual situations.

Books by Michelle A. Valentine

The Black Falcon Series

ROCK THE BEGINNING
Included in the Complete Series Collection
ROCK THE HEART
ROCK THE BAND
ROCK MY BED
ROCK MY WORLD
ROCK THE BEAT
ROCK MY BODY
COMPLETE SERIES COLLECTION

Hard Knocks Series

PHENOMENAL X
COMING SOON–XAVIER COLD

The Collectors Series

DEMON AT MY DOOR
COMING SOON—DEMON IN MY BED

A Sexy Manhattan Fairytale

NAUGHTY KING
Thank you for reading Naughty King.
Please consider leaving an honest review.
COMING SOON—FIESTY PRINCESS
COMING SOON—DIRTY ROYALS

Wicked White Series

WICKED WHITE (Releases June 23rd 2015)

A SEXY MANHATTAN FAIRYTALE: PART ONE

Michelle A. Valentine

Chapter I
THE CURSE

Alexander

I stare down at the woman on her knees in front of me. Her eager hands work quickly to undo my belt then they move on to my zipper.

She tosses her blonde hair back and grins. "I'm gonna suck your cock so good, baby, you'll be begging for more."

I thread my fingers through her mass of curls and fist them, forcing her to look up at me. "Coming in your mouth has a two hundred dollar price tag. You'll do the job I paid for, and then you'll get the fuck out. I'll want nothing more to do with you after that. Understand?"

She narrows her brown eyes at me. At first, I think this one might actually have a little backbone to her, and may just tell me to go to hell like I deserve, but she doesn't. They never do. Instead, she gets right to work rubbing my semi-hard cock through my boxer-briefs.

The only thing women see when they are in my presence is money—I'm surrounded by it. They see the material shit I have and their eyes light up like they've just found their golden fucking goose.

It's been both a curse and a blessing since I was twenty years old and inherited my father's billions. Every single woman I've ever been with has convinced herself that she'd be the one to tame me. That her magical pussy would make me fall madly in love with her—that I'd marry her and sign over half of my fortune.

Not fucking likely.

I know this looks bad. Most people would be both disgusted and curious as to why a devastatingly handsome, shrewd, successful businessman like myself would stoop to hiring a hooker. Truth is? It's fucking convenient. I send a text, and I get whatever I'm in the mood for. No questions asked.

That's why for the past few months I've relied on paying for escorts from a discreet service. It's less hassle than trying to find a slutty socialite to bang. I did that for two years straight, and it created more work for me than the lay was worth because I had to deal with kicking their annoying asses out the next day.

That shit gets exhausting.

The blonde reaches down inside my shorts and then shoves them down, resting the waistband under my ball sack. There's a wicked gleam in her eyes as she licks her lips and then pops my head into her mouth.

Now we're fucking getting somewhere.

The bitch goes to work licking, sucking, and deep-throating my cock. Her saliva coats my shaft, and I lean my head back against the leather couch in my office as I finally start enjoying what I've paid for.

There's nothing like a blowjob to start my day off right.

The handle on my office door moves, and my head snaps up just in time to make direct eye contact with my new secretary, Margo, as she steps into my office, unannounced, closing the door behind her. She's been doing that for the past two days. This girl needs to fucking learn how to knock before she comes waltzing in here. I'm about to teach her that lesson right now.

I fully expect my mousy new employee's cheeks to flush as she rushes from my office, but she surprises me as she stands there, only allowing her mouth to fall open as she takes in the sight of the woman pleasing me.

The blonde attempts to stop, but I'm enjoying making Margo uncomfortable, so I place my hand on the back of her head and order, "Don't you dare fucking stop."

Margo gasps, raising a well-manicured hand to her pouty lips while her blue eyes widen behind her dark-rimmed glasses.

It takes her a minute, but when she turns to leave, I have a different idea in mind. "Margo, if you walk out of that door, you're fired."

She halts mid-step at my domineering command. She needs this job. She and I both know it.

Margo smoothes back her black hair which is still perfectly in place in her uptight bun, and slowly turns back around to face me. "Why do you want me in here?"

I give her my cockiest shit-eatin' grin. "Because I want to stare at you while I come in this bitch's mouth."

She shakes her head. "This is absolutely insane. I'm not going—"

"You *will* stay," I order again. "Because if you don't, I'll make a phone call to Daddy and tell him that our little deal is off. Your call, princess."

She folds her arms over her chest, and I raise my eyebrow in challenge to her. That bitch honestly thinks she's better than I am. She's so uptight and highfalutin. Ever since she walked in here two days ago, I've wanted nothing more than to break her. I've been thinking of creative ways to show Margo that I run shit around here, and that the only reason I've even allowed her to have a job in my office is because her father begged me. Part of the deal to buy out his company included that she'd have a secure job.

Margo needs to know that I'm her new daddy. She's no longer the princess of a million-dollar empire because as soon as I ink this deal to bail her father out, I'll own her, just like I'll own her family's business.

I lick my lips while I wait on Margo to make her move. Her eyes flit down to my mouth and then down to the blonde who is now gagging herself to please me.

I lift my hips off the couch as I hold the blonde's head in place and fuck her mouth while Margo watches me.

Margo's chest heaves and my eyes are drawn to the tops of her tits mounding out of the top of her blouse.

I quickly close my eyes because I don't want to think about Margo's tits, but for some strange reason, I can't stop. Suddenly, it isn't some random prostitute sucking me off. It's uptight Margo in her naughty wannabe schoolteacher outfit.

I slide my teeth along my bottom lip then bite down as I suck in a quick breath. My eyes snap open, making direct eye contact with Margo as I come hard, shooting my load down the blonde's throat as my employee watches with a scowl on her face.

A shudder rips through me as I bask in the afterglow of one fine orgasm. I smile as the blonde unwraps her mouth from my cock and licks the tip of my dick to make sure she swallows down every last bit of come.

Margo continues to shoot daggers at me. This is all kinds of wrong and a fucking sexual harassment lawsuit waiting to happen, but I honestly don't give a shit.

All I care about is making sure my point is crystal clear with my new bitch of an employee—she is here to serve me. Not the other way around.

I sit up, stuffing my cock back inside my underwear before zipping my pants up. "Margo, pay the lady."

Margo's plump lip curls in what I'm sure is an expression of thorough disgust. "Pay for your own fucking whores."

Her words shock me at first, but then I find myself highly amused. I burst out in a deep laugh, which only makes Margo's face even redder before I fish my wallet from my back pocket. I lay two hundred-dollar bills on my knee for the hooker while never taking my eyes from my heated secretary. "You're free to leave now."

Relief floods Margo's face as she turns, but I stop her. "Not you, Margo. I was talking to my . . . *guest* here."

The hooker stuffs the money down in her bra and then winks. "You tasted yummy. Request me anytime."

Margo rolls her eyes behind the woman and shakes her head, but I simply nod at the woman. "What was your name again?"

"Candy." She grins.

"Of course it is," Margo scoffs.

I push myself up from the couch and button my jacket, putting myself back together. "Sorry, Candy. I never request the same girl twice. More than once and you bitches get clingy and forget I hired you just to get me off, not to talk. Matter of fact—" I glance down at my watch. "—it's time for you to get the fuck out. I've got a meeting to prepare for."

Candy's nostrils flare. "You can't treat people like this."

"Of course, I can. I'm Alexander King, and I can do whatever the fuck I please. Now leave before I call security and have you forcibly removed from the property."

"Asshole," Candy calls over her shoulder as she leaves without another word of protest.

You would think being called that would cause me to flinch, but no, I revel in the name. I like that women hate the way I treat them. It ensures they keep their distance.

The door slams and Margo points her gaze in my direction. "I assume you're done with me now that the show's over?"

Since we're alone, I take my time to rake my eyes over Margo. She still appears angry enough to chop my dick off.

Good.

I want her to hate me.

I want to make it clear that we are not friends.

"Margo . . ." I can't help smirking as I adjust the cuff of my jacket. "I'm just getting started with you."

She arches a perfectly manicured eyebrow. "What's that supposed to mean?"

I laugh. "You seem like a bright girl—I mean, not just anyone earns two degrees from Harvard. You know that sooner or later you'll be on your knees before me."

She laughs bitterly. "You can't be serious. I would never be one of your two-dollar whores."

I take a step toward her, reducing the gap between us to mere inches. She's close enough that I can feel her breath coming out in warm little puffs. "Don't pretend like that didn't turn you on. I saw you watching—waiting your turn like a good girl. Don't worry, you'll get your chance someday."

"Fuck you," she spats.

"Not yet, but you will." I trace the exposed flesh on her chest with the tip of my finger. "You'll beg me for it. You'll beg me to fuck you, hoping that it'll be you who changes my asshole ways and makes me fall in love." She opens her mouth to protest, but I press my finger to her lips, cutting her off. "You will. I have that effect on women, but you're smart enough to know that if you do that—if you let me have you—you'll quit when you don't get your way like the spoiled little brat your father has raised. And we both know that you quitting will piss off Daddy, don't we?"

"I needed a secure job that will pay the bills after my family goes bankrupt. You know that. It's part of the deal with my father," she argues, but I'm not stupid enough to buy into that.

"Don't lie to me," I scold her roughly, and she stiffens. "We're both highly intelligent human beings so let's not play dumb. You're here to spy on me—to figure out a way to stop me from buying your father's company for pennies and then sell off everything he's worked for piece by fucking piece, in turn making me an even richer man."

She lifts her chin. "You're a bastard, you know that?"

I shrug. "Maybe so, but I'm honest and just to show you that infiltrating my business doesn't scare me one damn bit, I'm going to allow you to stay. But know this: I'm going to make your life a living hell while you're here. I'll have you dying to fuck my brains out or needing to walk away before you kill me with your own bare hands. Either way—you're fucked."

Margo takes a deep breath and closes her eyes, giving me a chance to study her features. She wears the dark hair on her head pulled back, but I imagine that when she lets it down, it hangs in long loose waves around her shoulders. When she opens her eyes and gazes up at me, I notice the blue of her eyes standing out against the contrast of her dark hair, and it hits me—I bet she'd be an amazing lay.

She licks her lips, not in a way that's meant to be sexy but in the way people do when they're nervous, and my eyes are instantly drawn to her mouth.

Dammit all to hell. This would be so much easier if she was ugly—to humiliate her by playing with her emotions and knowing there'd be no way in hell I would actually fuck her except out of spite. The problem is that's not the case. She's exactly my favorite type of woman to fuck: beautiful and bitchy. When I take her, I can't allow myself to enjoy it. I won't give her that satisfaction.

Margo stares at me for a long moment, and just when I think she's about to lay into me again, she twists her hand around my tie, yanking me closer. Without warning her tongue darts out and touches my top lip, causing a tiny shudder to tear through me before she pulls back with a sly smile on her face. "That's where you're wrong, Mr. King. That prediction implies that I would actually fall for your juvenile antics of seduction." Her hand presses against my chest and then moves down to my stomach, drifting even farther south. "Those boyish tricks would never work on me. I'm a woman who always gets what she wants." I let out a low grunt of half pain and half excitement as she grabs my semi-hard cock through my slacks. Stilling her hand on my cock, she leans into my ear and whispers, "When I want it." The urge to throw her onto my desk and fuck her senseless surges through me. Never has a woman asserted herself with me, and as much as I fucking hate to admit it, I'm totally turned on by it.

Margo kisses my cheek before she pulls back and releases a hearty laugh. "Who's fucked now?"

Angry that I allowed myself to be distracted for one moment, I shove her away a little rougher than I mean to. "Get the fuck out. We're done here."

Margo laughs as she takes a step back toward the door. "Oh, Mr. King, that's where you're wrong again. We both know this little game of ours has only just begun."

"I said we're fucking done with this conversation." I glare at her.

"As you wish." She smirks and actually fucking curtsies before heading out my door, invoking my hatred even more.

The moment the door closes, I plop down in my chair and loosen my tie. How in the holy hell did that just happen?

My nostrils flare and I take a deep breath, trying to maintain my composure and not throw something. The one thing I fucking hate is to be shown up. I'm always the winner—number one at all times. She will not take control of this situation.

No fucking way.

I won't allow that to happen. Ever.

If Margo Buchanan wants a fucking war with me then, a war is what she's going to fucking get.

Chapter II
DIRTY LAUNDRY

Alexander

The door to my office opens and I scowl, fully expecting Margo to waltz back in for round two. I relax when Jack walks through the door instead.

His neatly trimmed dark hair matches his pressed black suit. Jack hasn't looked in my direction yet to see my utter disarray because he's too busy running his hand through his hair and staring at my man-eater secretary.

When the door shuts behind him, Jack's wearing the biggest shit-eatin' grin known to mankind. "Damn. You didn't tell me that you hired a new hot piece of ass. Have you tapped that yet, or do I still have a shot at getting in there before you? You know how I fucking hate your sloppy seconds."

I roll my eyes. "Brother, if I were you, I wouldn't touch that bitch with a double-bagged dick. She's fuckin' trouble."

Jack's face lights up as he glances back at the door before turning back to me, wiggling his eyebrows over his dark eyes. "My favorite kind."

Oh, shit. I've just enticed him even more. Jack has been my wingman for a long time, and I know he's just as smooth with the ladies as I am. If he sets his sights on Margo, he won't give up until he's fucked her seven ways till Sunday.

I've got to correct this situation stat. Throw a little ice water on him, so-to-speak, before he goes getting any crazy ideas like asking her out.

"She's Dan Buchanan's daughter," I quickly inform him before he has a chance to get a full-on chub thinking about how damn hot Margo looks sitting out there on the other side of that door.

Jack's eyes widen. "No fucking way! Buchanan produced that? I don't believe it."

I lean back in my chair and straighten my tie. "Afraid so."

"So what's she doing here? When you said you'd give her a job, I didn't expect it to be as *your* assistant. Doesn't she know that we're about to dismantle her father's business and sell it for parts? She should hate our guts, not be out there working for the enemy."

I nod. "She knows, and it's the very reason she's here. The last time I met with Buchanan, as you know, he only agreed to sell me Buchanan Industries if I promised to give his darling daughter a job, so I figured I'd put her where I'd be able to keep my eye on her."

His brow furrows. "He can get her a job as a secretary anywhere."

"He was afraid that since she's a new grad, she'd have a tough time finding something that paid well in this economy."

He shakes his head. "I still don't understand why make it part of the deal that she has to work here for you?"

I drum my fingers on the desk. "Think about it, Jack. Buchanan is a crafty old son-of-a-bitch. He's going to fight tooth and nail to figure out a way to save his business. By getting his daughter in here, he figures he'll be able to get info about the buyers we have lined up and cut us off at the pass. Then he'll try to make a deal with them first to sell off pieces of his company that are easily discarded, leaving him with less overhead and keeping him afloat until he can figure out his next move."

"And you agreed to let her come here knowing that? Shit, Alexander. She could ruin everything." I hear the edge in Jack's voice. He's never been one to keep a cool head when he stresses. "We've got billions riding on this deal. You have to become the activist shareholder in Buchanan Industries."

I hold up my hand, stopping him before he even gets started. "Relax, Jack. I have this under control. Do you honestly think that Margo Buchanan is a match for me? Come on, man. You've known me for how long now?"

He shakes his head. "You're right. I do know you, which means I know that women are your fucking kryptonite. Face it; you've been in a rut for a couple of years now. Hell, you've not been the same since Jess fucked you over. You haven't been with a woman longer than one night since her. If Margo wags her hot ass in front of you, you'll leap, my friend, and your self-control will be flushed down the fucking toilet. She'll get in your head, and this whole deal will be fucked."

I know Jack thinks that I've hit a dry spell since Jess Fontaine left me for another man two years ago—that she crushed me—but he couldn't be more wrong. Jess taking off with some tennis pro she met at the country club only hardened me more. It made me stronger—made me realize that love really doesn't exist. It's just this thing people created to comfort themselves within stories—a mythical thing like Santa Claus and the Easter Bunny. I learned a long time ago that fairy tales don't exist. People need to stop wasting their time searching for something that isn't real.

Paying for pussy is definitely the way to go.

So Jack needs to stop worrying about me. Margo Buchanan will not get to me no matter how tempting she may be.

I chuckle. "Trust me. That's not going to happen."

"Make sure it doesn't. We need Buchanan to sell you his shares. Our Japanese connections want pieces of his company, and the only way we can make that happen is if you're the main shareholder. We can't afford for anything to go wrong."

"You've got to stop worrying. You're going to make yourself old and gray far too soon." I push myself away from the desk and walk over to the small bar that's in my office. The crystal decanter holding my favorite thirty-year-old scotch clinks against the glass as I pour the amber liquid. "Come have a drink with me. Let's celebrate our victory before we close this deal over lunch."

Jack walks over and lays a couple of papers on the wooden bar. "I've got the latest numbers on the Buchanan stock. It's down thirty points. Everything is lining up for us perfectly. We're on the road to making our biggest deal yet. Your father would've been proud."

I hand Jack his glass as I smile at the thought of my father. It pleases me immensely to know that if he were here, Father would be partaking in this celebratory drink. Fucking cancer. It took him away from me much too soon, forcing me to grow up way too fast.

I tip the glass back and down my drink before pouring myself another. I need a fucking subject change. "I heard a rumor about you."

Jack's eyebrow arches. "Me? From whom?"

I smirk. "One guess."

"Fucking Diem." Jack rubs the back of his neck. "What did your darling sister tell you about me now?"

I laugh. "Rachel Winslet, Jack? Really? How fucking desperate were you to take that home?"

"Dammit," Jack mutters. "I was at a benefit at the Waldorf, and I had one too many to drink. I spent most of the night talking to your sister. When it was time to find someone to share in the pleasure of my company for the evening, all the good women were taken. Rachel was my only willing body."

"Her body's always willing," I say, and then laugh, unable to hold it back.

Jack shrugs, like it's there's nothing else he can say. It's a well-known fact that the woman is working her way through our social circles on her back.

I hold up my hands. "Hey, no judgment. A lay is a lay as long as you don't plan on taking it any further than that."

Jack tips back his glass and then sets it down on the bar. "Did Diem say anything else?"

I shake my head. "No, but what in the hell were you doing talking to my sister all night? You're not fucking her, are you? You know that's the one thing that would cause me to murder my best friend."

His face contorts, and his top lip curls. "It's not like that. You know we've always been friends. She's your little sister for Christ's sake."

"Well, what were the two of you doing together?"

"Diem and I were *just* talking."

"About what?" I ask a little agitated.

"Mainly . . . we were talking about you."

This causes my brow to furrow. "What the hell could possibly be so interesting about me that would cause the two of you to chat all evening?"

He shrugs. "She worries about you a lot. It's not healthy for you to work all the time and then spend your evenings alone."

I roll my eyes. "So you and Diem are experts on what's best for me now?"

"No. We just want to see you happy."

I level my stare on him. "Is anyone ever truly happy with their lives, Jack? The best someone can hope for is to have enough money not to be miserable in their existence until they die."

Jack sighs. "That's a pretty depressing outlook on life, man."

"Yeah, maybe, but it's an honest one. Seriously, you and Diem need to find more interesting topics of conversations."

He laughs. "What can I say? The King is a hot topic of conversation these days. It's hard to avoid talking about you when I'm out in public. I think you've pissed off over half of the females on the Upper East Side. They all say your name with such disdain that it's comical, and unfortunately, your sister and I are assholes by association. We've bonded through our pariah status. I would stop being your friend, but I like getting laid for being the nice guy out of our duo."

I chuckle. "Ah, so being the best friend of Manhattan's biggest prick has its perks?"

Jack fills his glass again and has a twinkle in his eye. "Sometimes."

A quick knock on my door catches my attention just as it swings open. Margo steps into my office and makes a big show of checking out the inside of the room before her eyes land on Jack. Her face lights up as she points a smile in his direction, and for some reason my shoulders stiffen.

"Do you need something, Margo?" I ask, drawing her attention away from Jack.

"I was just making sure that you were decent. The last time—" She smirks as her eyes flit over to Jack and then back to me "—I seemed to have come in at an inopportune moment when you had a guest in here."

Jack tilts his head, and I feel his gaze on me. I usually tell him everything—but admitting to your best friend that you buy sexual favors from high-paid escorts isn't something that I want to readily divulge to him.

Damn that Margo. She's doing this to get under my skin, but the fucking joke's going to be on her because I refuse to let this chick see me sweat.

I take a long drink and eye her over my glass. "Well, I'm glad that you've learned barging in without knocking is rude as fuck. At least you've learned one thing from me today."

She bites the corner of her lip. "I've learned plenty today."

"Glad to be of service. I always aim to please." I raise one eyebrow, daring her to say more in front of Jack, but she doesn't.

Instead, she glances down at the silver watch on her wrist. "You have a lunch meeting at twelve thirty and your car service is downstairs waiting."

I set my glass down. "Thank you, Margo. Be sure to bring your tablet and a notepad to take notes."

"I'm going?" I fight back a smile as I hear the surprise in her voice.

"Of course. That's what assistants do—they assist. I'll be ready in five and I expect you to be as well." I allow a hint of a smile to play along my lips as she stands there gaping at me. "That will be all, Margo."

I can tell that she doesn't like me dismissing her like common help, but something tells me that she doesn't want to make too big of a scene in front of Jack, so she doesn't mouth off before she turns and walks out of my office. The princess is definitely not used to anyone bossing her around.

This little game of ours is going to be fun.

The second the door closes, Jack scrubs his hand down his face. "Fuck. This isn't good."

"What?" I ask, unsure of what he's talking about.

He locks eyes with me. "Are you sure you haven't already fucked her?"

"No!" I argue. "I haven't touched her."

"Maybe not yet, but you will. I can see the way you two are looking at each other. It might be a hate fuck, but it's going to happen, and it's going to ruin everything we've worked for. She's part of her father's deal. Please, use the head on top of your shoulders because it has the smarter brain. It'll tell you that the best thing for business would be to *not* slip your dick in this chick."

I understand why he's flipping out. We have a lot of money riding on this, and with him being my company attorney, screwing this up will cause him a shit-ton of work on top of all the money King Corporation will lose. But he has to know that money and making sure that the company my father built succeeds is far more important than a piece of ass.

"Don't worry, Jack. I've got it all under control. I promise not to fuck the hired help." I put the crystal stopper back in the scotch decanter. "Now, let's head to lunch and see if we can get that bastard, Buchanan, to sign this deal."

I slap Jack on the back as I pass him and we head out to seal the deal and get Margo Buchanan the hell out of my office.

Margo

I cross my legs feeling Alexander King's cool gray eyes, which are set beneath a pair of dark eyebrows, taking in every inch of my exposed flesh. Even when I catch him staring, he doesn't seem the least bit apologetic. Rather than look away like most men would do in his position, he gives me one of those smart-ass smirks that I've grown accustomed to over the past few days since I started working for him, and he continues to stare at me blatantly.

The man is infuriating, and to make matters worse, he's impossibly good-looking. If I hadn't seen him in person, I would swear every picture I've ever seen of him had to have been airbrushed because no man ever looks that perfect all the time. But, sadly, Alexander is the exception. Everything about him draws me in. His Roman sculpted nose, chiseled cheekbones, and masculine jawline covered in a light beard—all of it fits exactly what I find attractive in a man to a T. It's a shame he's such a rat-bastard. Beauty is wasted on the wicked.

Infiltrating Alexander's business and seducing him in order to gain access to all the information my father needs is a far more difficult task than I had originally anticipated. Most men are all too eager to please me, but not Alexander. He's hell bent on making me miserable and teaching me what he deems as my place in this situation—below him. He has no idea that I'm not like most of these ridiculous Manhattan twits who run around here. His infamous name and hoards of wealth don't do a thing for me. He won't be able to walk all over me and use me as he does every other woman in our social circle. I'm pretty sure when I stood my ground earlier today it rattled him a bit, showing him that perhaps he's met his match with me.

"So, Ms. Buchanan, how do you like the job so far?" The deep voice beside me asks.

I turn toward Jack Sutherland, who I've quickly learned is one of the attorneys for the King Corporation and second in line for the biggest manwhore in Manhattan, behind none other than Alexander King. I can see why women throw themselves at Jack. Like Alexander, he's beautiful with his curly brown hair, hazel eyes, and adorable crooked grin. Though it seems to be a running theme that all well-polished men with model faces and insanely hot bodies are assholes. I swear there's a handbook somewhere that all attractive men are given, teaching them it's a must to be an egotistical womanizer who jump when any opportunity to stick their dick in something comes their way regardless of the consequences.

My mother constantly accuses me of trying to be the female version of Robin Hood. She thinks that I look for ways to punish men like these two for the sake of all womankind. I, on the other hand, always correct her and tell her that I simply won't allow jerks like Alexander King to gain the upper hand with me.

I will never allow a man to use me again. Once was enough of that bullshit.

Besides, someone needs to put these guys in their place from time to time.

I give Jack my most flirty smile, doing the best I can to win him over. God knows I don't need him breathing down my neck for being here like Alexander did earlier. "It's been a real eye-opening experience. There's obviously a lot for me to learn since this is my first job, but I tend to catch on to things very quickly."

Jack's eyes dart down to my mouth for a split second before he reconnects his gaze with mine, and he grins. "I love a woman who's a quick study. Where did you graduate?"

"Harvard," I answer, and it causes him to raise his eyebrows.

"Really? Wow. That's impressive. What was your major?"

"I double majored in finance and pre-law and graduated with honors. I wanted to keep my options open."

"Wow. I must say, Ms. Buchanan, that's amazing. Old King here had better be on his toes when it comes to you. You seem like a highly intelligent woman." I revel in his compliments as I thank him because I'm damn proud of my education. I earned that completely on my own merit.

I love my mother to pieces, but I never wanted to be like her when I got older. She's beautiful, which is exactly what caught my father's eye years ago. My mother married into wealth, became accustomed to the lifestyle, and when my father divorced her, she was desperate to find another wealthy man to take his place. I always told myself that I wanted to be a woman who stood on her own two feet—a woman who didn't need a man to complete her or her bank account.

And believe it or not, in this day and age, a determined woman intimidates the shit out of most men.

My deep-seated drive to succeed came out in full force today. It gave me the courage to rattle the unshakable Alexander King this morning. Of course I knew the little show he put on for me with the skanky bottle-blond hooker was meant to send me running for the hills, and while it turned my stomach to see such a disgusting display, I decided I wasn't going to make getting rid of me so easy for him.

"Do you think you'll make a permanent home with us at King, or are you using the position as a mode to gain experience?" Jack asks, jerking me away from my thoughts.

I glance over at Alexander, who is watching me intently as if he's studying his prey. It's as if he's just waiting for me to say the wrong thing so he can attack.

"So far I love how kind everyone has been to me. This would be an amazing company to work for long-term. I guess we'll have to wait to see if I screw up around here before I can make any predictions on how long I'll stay. Mr. King may fire me."

Jack chuckles. "I doubt he'll be allowing you to go anywhere anytime soon. You're already far too important for him to ever entertain the idea of letting you go over simple on-the-job mistakes."

"That's very kind of you," I tell him as I glance over at Alexander again. "Hopefully, he decides to keep me around for a while."

The cool smile playing on Alexander's lips is difficult to read, but if I had to guess from our previous conversation, that annoyingly charming expression only reiterates his feelings from earlier. He won't get rid of me, but he's going to do his damnedest to make sure I leave on my own. Well, I have news for him.

Game on, motherfucker.

Chapter IV
UNEXPECTED COMPLICATION

Alexander

Sitting across from Dan Buchanan in this upscale restaurant, I take in his stern expression that's intended to intimidate me and smile. Buchanan means to display worldly knowledge with his gray hair and multitude of wrinkles, but I know better. This man may have been a shrewd businessman at one time in his life, but not anymore. Being the sole contractor for building mini-bird helicopters for the U.S. military, he's allowed the wealth he's earned over the years to cloud his sound judgment making in both his personal and business finances, which is exactly what landed him with a company that's about to fold. I've done my homework on him, just like I do on all my targets. It makes the kill that much easier when I know their weaknesses.

Jack slides the contract across the table to Buchanan. "Here's the contract of sale, as requested. I figured we'd get the paperwork exchange out of the way so we can enjoy lunch."

Buchanan's weasel-dick attorney, Seth James, picks up the document and examines a few lines of it. "We'll look over it and let you know."

"Keep in mind," I interject, "that I already own nearly half the stock in Buchanan Industries. I'm close to being a majority shareholder, and I assure you that will help sway the board in my favor when they see my plan of action to save this sinking ship of a business."

Buchanan slams his fist down on the table. "Selling our technologies to another country is out of the question."

I lean forward, resting an elbow on the table. "Regardless of your personal feelings in the matter, selling parts of the business is what's best, and that is exactly what's going to happen."

"No," he growls. "I won't allow that to happen. I'll find a way to buy my stock back from you."

I set my gaze on him. "That's not going to happen. You can't afford it and you've already exhausted all your lines of credit to keep the company running long enough to fill the last order you received from the Navy for mini choppers. Face it, Mr. Buchanan. It's over. Your fate now rests in my hands."

Buchanan and I continue to stare each other down. I love the challenge in his eyes. Neither of us saying a word while our colleagues, plus his daughter, watch us intently—all of them feeling the tension too. Buchanan absolutely loathes me. I can tell, and I fucking love it.

He doesn't want to let his baby go. I get that. It's been his company for a very long time now, but he needs to understand that it cannot be saved. He's in far too much debt, and he just needs to come to the realization that I'm going to end up with it to do as I please.

This is the most tense lunch I've ever attended even though Jack lectured me about keeping this meeting social.

"Good afternoon," the male waiter dressed in a fitted black suit greets us when he approaches the table. "I am Gerald, and I'll be your waiter this afternoon. May I start you off with some drinks?"

"Scotch on the rocks for me," I say when he directs his attention to me.

"Water, please," Margo answers when the waiter's eyes expectantly zero in on her.

"I'll have a scotch as well, and be sure to bring out bread with lots of butter," Buchanan orders and then dismisses the waiter after everyone else has requested their beverages.

"Daddy!" Margo complains. "You know what the doctor said. Diabetics need to lay off the bread."

Buchanan gives his daughter a half-sided smile, and it immediately brings the tension around us down a notch. Perhaps it wasn't a bad idea to bring her along after all. "I know, darling, and I have been, but a man needs to splurge every now and again. It keeps us sane."

Margo rolls those magnetic blue eyes of hers and sighs. "I really don't get why you men always want to do things that are so bad for you."

"It's in our nature," he lectures. "All men have their own way of cutting loose."

Her gaze darts over to me. "Isn't that the truth."

It's hard not to laugh like a schoolgirl with the pure satisfaction I feel knowing that I'm getting to her, but I try to remain stoic without much luck. A ghost of a smile hints at my lips.

"Alexander, did you see this?" Jack asks as he slides his phone over to me.

An email from Yamada Enterprises' president sits on the screen. My eyes race over the words, knowing Jack wouldn't be showing me this now if it weren't important since this is our interested buyer in the Buchanan deal.

I sigh heavily. "Gentlemen, it seems that you'll have a bit of an extension in reviewing the contract. My business contact for the deal has requested that I meet with him face to face while he is in the states vacationing in Las Vegas. Mr. Sutherland and I will be leaving at the end of the week and will return on Monday—"

"I can't do that, Alexander," Jack says next to me. "It's my . . . cousin's wedding and I just can't miss it."

My lips twist. This isn't like Jack. First off, he's never interrupted me in the middle of something, and second, when did he start giving a fuck about some random cousin who he's never talked about until now?

"Who cares," I say. "I'm missing my sister's twenty-fourth birthday party. This is business. Skip it."

Jack frowns. "I can't. There's no way I can get out of this one."

Before I have a chance to fire off more reasons of why Jack should stop being a pussy and go to this meeting, Margo's voice cuts between us. "I'll go with you. I am your assistant, after all."

My eyes widen. The thought of being alone in Vegas, of all fucking places, with this woman, causes my dick to twitch. I can't be around her that long and not fuck her. It'll drive me out of my mind.

"That's a great idea, Margo," Buchanan chimes in. "You can make sure whoever is getting this company is worthy. It would be nice for you to make a few contacts."

I hold up my hand. "Wait, just a minute. This is my deal, and I don't think—"

"It'll still be your baby," Margo purrs next to me. "I promise not to interfere in any way. I just want to learn. After all, you're known around this city for being able to charm the pants off anyone you set your sights on. I think I can learn a lot by watching you in action."

"Oh, you'll see me in action, all right." I purse my lips and cut myself off, not wanting to say crude things to her in front of her father and fuck up this deal.

Fuck.

I sigh while both Margo and her father watch me intently, waiting for me to give in and take the enemy along with me. The information Margo could gain from this trip could be devastating to the deal, but I doubt they'll be able to negotiate a better deal for Buchanan Industries with Yamada Enterprises. I have nothing to worry about by allowing her to tag along, and it'll make Buchanan still feel comfortable that he has gained the upper hand on me because his sweet ball-breaking daughter is his little spy.

"Fine," I concede. "Margo can go, but once we get back, we put this deal to bed. Agreed?"

Buchanan nods. "Agreed. I'll have my answer for you by then."

I roll my shoulders and relax a bit in my chair. Spend the weekend with Margo in Sin City—no problem. I can get through this.

Chapter V
COUNTDOWN

Margo

Why couldn't Alexander King be a pudgy, fifty-something, bald man with bad breath? It would make it a whole lot easier to pretend that I don't feel the weight of his stare on me every time I go into his office if he were hideously ugly. As it stands now, it's hard for my body not to respond to him. It's like I have this visceral reaction to him whenever I'm in his presence, and that scares the shit out of me.

His advances had backed off a bit from a couple of days ago when I caught the hooker blowing him in his office. Thank God. But I can tell he's ready to make good on his promise to have me beg him to fuck me. He thinks fucking him will break me—that I'm some little twit who wears her heart on her sleeve—and that pisses me off. *He* pisses me off.

The countdown to Vegas is on. In just one day, I'll be on a private plane heading across the country to the biggest adult playground in the world. I don't know how being alone with him for an entire weekend is going to go. He was probably right. I'll want to either fuck him or kill him with my own bare hands, but I guess it will be the latter.

"Margo?" Alexander's voice rings through the intercom sitting on my desk.

"Yes, Mr. King," I answer with as much professionalism as I can muster.

He quickly rattles off a list of tasks for me. "I need the daily stock report on Buchanan Industries, a dinner reservation for two at Per Se for seven tonight, and my coffee cup is empty."

Out of all the things that he asks me to do, getting his coffee irritates me the most. Why in the hell do I have to fetch it? Are his legs fucking broken?

I sigh before plastering on a huge smile that will come through in the tone of my voice as I press the speaker button. "Right away, sir."

The stock report and coffee are the easy things on the list, but securing a table at Per Se took some finagling. After I had disclosed exactly which Mr. King was requesting the table, it went rather smoothly. Seems his name has quite the pull.

I carry the report and coffee into his office. He holds his hand out for the paper as I set the mug on his desk.

I hope he fucking chokes on it.

I begin to turn away, but his voice quickly halts me. "I didn't dismiss you yet, Margo."

My nostrils flare as I spin back around to face him. "Will there be anything else, sir?"

Alexander pushes himself out of the chair and smoothes his red tie, attracting my attention to the definition hiding behind that blue buttoned-down dress shirt. I've noticed that when he's working in his office, he removes his jacket. It almost makes him appear casual and more approachable, but I know better. He's still an uptight asshole with or without the jacket.

He walks around the desk and stops in front of me before leaning back against the expensive-looking mahogany desk. "Are you all prepared for our trip to Vegas?"

I nod. "Yes. I mean, I will be once I finish packing—"

He shakes his head and a strand of dark hair falls across his forehead. My fingers itch to reach up and shove it back into place. I wonder if it's as soft as it looks.

Stop it! You cannot be thinking about touching this man. He is the enemy and a complete asshole. Get a hold of yourself. Don't allow hormones to take control.

"I don't mean your personal items, Margo. I meant do you have all of the necessary tasks designated to the support staff to cover in our absence."

I bite the inside of my lower lip as it occurs to me that doing that hadn't crossed my mind. "I didn't think that was necessary since tomorrow is Friday. We'll be back in the office by Tuesday, so I just planned to return calls then."

Alexander studies me intently as he taps his index finger against the smooth wood of his desk. "Time is always of the essence—it's even more valuable in my line of work. One missed tip on an investment could cost billions."

I swallow hard as the complexity of my mistake becomes clear. "I'll make sure Jack's secretary fields all of my calls and notifies me if something is urgent."

I have to keep shit together and up my game. While working for King Enterprises isn't my real career aspiration, I can still learn a lot while I'm here—things that can help me once I've found my job niche.

He straightens the cuff of his shirt. "Have a car pick you up tomorrow promptly at eight. The private jet leaves at nine. Apparently the Yamada family has requested my presence at a pool party at the Hard Rock at two, and I'll expect you to accompany me."

My eyes widen. "You can't possibly expect me to attend a meeting in a swimsuit! That's . . . no . . . it's ridiculous."

"It's not up for discussion." His voice rings with authority. "You want this job—you play the fucking game and be a good fucking sport while we meet with my business contacts."

I open my mouth to lash out and tell him that there's no way on God's green earth that I'll be parading around in front of him in a bikini, but the moment he arches his eyebrow, I quickly decide against it. My father will be so pissed if I screw this up. He's counting on me to schmooze this contact of Alexander's so that they'll go to my father directly and make a deal for whatever part of Buchanan Industries they're after.

"Fine, but just don't expect me to become one of your paid whores while we're there. This is just business."

A playful smirk flirts across his full lips. "I like this tough act of yours—the way you're fighting against me. It will make the moment your lips are wrapped around my cock that much more enjoyable, Margo."

I release a bitter laugh, and it fills the inside of his office. "Those suave lines may work on the women you're used to dealing with, but I assure you, it'll take more than a few pretty words and a bunch of heady stares to turn my head. I don't date assholes."

"But do you fuck 'em? That's the question of the hour, isn't it? I don't ever remember promising you that we'd date. I said we'd fuck. Dating versus fucking is two very distinctly different things."

I narrow my gaze. "That's never going to happen."

"We'll see."

We stand there staring at one another. Neither one of us says a word. I don't know what it is about this man, but he brings out the competitive nature in me like no other. We are at an impasse—both wanting our ways. I need information to help my father, and he wants to destroy me with sex, causing me to tuck my tail between my legs in embarrassment. I don't see either one of us conceding, so the best that I can hope for is whatever happens in Vegas to tip the scales in my favor and allow me to get the inside advantage that I need.

Chapter VI
BROTHER KNOWS BEST

Alexander

I glance down at my watch and sigh. Diem being late shouldn't surprise me. After all, I've known her for officially twenty-four years this weekend, so Diem being late for her own birthday dinner is a given. That girl couldn't be on time to save her life. Dad knew that about her too, which is why he left his business to me. He knew Diem was too much of a free spirit to ever be mixed up in the corporate life.

As I pick up my cell to call her again to ask her where she is, she comes bounding up to the table with the biggest smile on her face, making her green eyes brighten and accentuating the emerald shade of the dress she's wearing.

"You're late," I scold her.

Diem waves me off dismissively as the maitre d' pulls out the chair for her. She tucks a blond strand of hair behind her ear before she makes eye contact with me. "Stop being such a stiff. I wasn't that late. Besides, I have a really good excuse this time."

Staying mad at my baby sister is virtually impossible. It's odd how she got on my very last nerve when I was younger, but after my father died that annoyance fell away and all I wanted to do was protect her. I had to become the man of the family at twenty. When my bitch of a mother decided taking care of an ill man with cancer and her then fourteen-year-old daughter was no longer *her thing,* I became responsible for Diem.

"What's the exciting news?" I give in and ask because I can tell by the expression on her face that she's bursting at the seams to tell me something.

Her smile widens. "I sold a painting!"

"You did?" Now the little shit has me grinning like a fool. "That's excellent news. Which piece did they buy? The self-portrait?"

Her eyes widen and the smile drops from her face. "How did you know?"

I lean back, pleased that not only do I have a mind for business, but an eye for art as well. "I know good work when I see it, and that was your best work to date. It finally made me realize that sending you to that ridiculously expensive art school wasn't a complete waste of money."

Diem rolls her eyes at me. "Don't even act like the money was ever an issue. Besides, going to that school was my dream."

I sigh. "I know it was, and even though I don't say it often enough, I'm proud of you. I'm glad you have aspirations and goals, even if they don't necessarily align with the educational direction I wanted for you."

She unfolds the white cloth napkin on the table and drapes it across her lap. "Not all of us mere mortals can become cut-throat business moguls like you."

I smirk at her sassy tone as I reach into the inside pocket of my jacket and pull out the blue box containing her gift. "I shouldn't give you this for that little quip, but because I don't want to hear you complain that I didn't get you anything . . . here you go."

I slide the box across the table toward her. "Happy birthday, Diem."

She places her hand on the box while her shoulders slump forward and her mouth draws into a pout. "Are you sure you have to go away this weekend? My party is going to be epic."

"Afraid so," I tell her. "Yamada is in the States, living it up in Vegas, and I have to meet up with him to secure a deal I'm working on."

She raises her eyebrows. "Now I know exactly why you don't want to cancel. You and Yamada back together again? I smell trouble brewing."

I chuckle and shake my head. "Trust me. Those days are long over with. Besides, I'm taking my new secretary to make sure things stay strictly professional and I don't get distracted."

"Margo Buchanan? The Feisty Princess? She's your new secretary, right? I think taking her will cloud your judgment, and I know she'll definitely be a distraction to Yamada."

"The Feisty *what?*" I furrow my brow. "How do you know about her?"

This is news to me. How in the hell does my baby sister always seem to be in the know about everything in this town?

"Everyone calls her that." She pauses for a beat and then shrugs. "Jack told me about her working for you. The whole Upper East Side is buzzing about it. I remember Margo from high school. She was a grade ahead of me. She's beautiful, smart, and vicious when it comes to getting what she wants but loyal to the core in respects to the people she loves, or at least that's what the word is. She's kind of like the female version of you."

Diem giggles, and I hate the fact that my sister seems to know more about Margo than I do. I don't like thinking about Margo because it either pisses me off or makes me horny as hell every time I do.

I need a subject change.

My lips twist. "I don't think I like you and Jack talking so much."

"Why?" she fires back.

"Because, Diem, he's my best friend, and it's . . . I . . . it's just asking for trouble." I grab the glass of water in front of me and take a big gulp, unsure of why I'm allowing myself to get all tongue tied.

"We're just friends, Alexander. It is possible for a man and a woman to just hang out from time to time without anything else going on."

"No, it's not."

"You're taking Margo to Vegas so doesn't that make her your friend?"

"No, it doesn't. She hates me. We definitely are not friends," I tell her.

Diem frowns. "You should do something about that if you want this business arrangement to work out with her. You know Dad always taught us that you catch more bees with honey."

Diem's right. Father always said that, and he was known around this city for being a fair and honest man. Unfortunately, I couldn't use his methods when I took over. I was far too young at twenty to be taken seriously at running a billion-dollar company, which is why I had to be tough—flex my muscle—and show people that I wouldn't be fucked with.

I lean back in my chair and loosen my tie a bit. Maybe my sister has a point. Being a total dick to Margo doesn't seem to be making any headway. "What do you suppose I do? Concede and let her win—let her think I'm a pushover? I can't do that, Diem. It's not in me to allow someone to get the best of me."

She shakes her head. "I'm not saying to instantly become a pussy. I'm just saying to lighten up a bit. I know how you get when you think someone is your enemy. You become set on destroying them. Margo might not be as bad as you have her made out to be in your head."

"Or she could be much worse," I answer instantly.

"I doubt that. No one is a bigger badass than you." Diem winks and then laughs. "I think you should just try to be a little nicer. Break through her walls a little and show her that you pay attention. It'll make this business deal a lot more pleasant for both of you. This should be stress-free because you already have Yamada in the bag. Nothing Margo Buchanan can do will change that so you might as well learn to get along with her."

My fingers run across my bearded jawline and I sigh. "When did you get so smart?"

She grins. "Turning twenty-four will do that to you. Speaking of that, let's see what you got me." Her fingers work nimbly to tear open the Tiffany's box to reveal the diamond charm bracelet I bought for her. Her fingers slide over the engraving as she reads it aloud. "Love you, Squirt."

She wrinkles her nose.

I laugh, loving that she still hates the nickname I gave her when we were just kids but won't throw it back at me because of all the sparkly diamonds surrounding the name.

I pick up my drink. "Happy birthday, Squirt."

Chapter VII
NO ESCAPE

Margo

Right on time, the black Town Car pulls up to take me to King's private jet. Riding in private planes is nothing new to me, seeing as how my father's company specializes in building aircrafts. It is, however, the first time I've ever taken a cross-country flight accompanying a man who I absolutely loath.

My cell rings and I dig through my handbag to find it. I smile when I see Mother's name flash across the screen. "Hello, Mother."

"Gah," she sighs into the phone. "How many times have I asked you to call me Lily? You know I don't like people thinking that I'm old enough to be your mother."

I laugh. "I hate to be the one to break it to you, but I think the tabloids exposed that secret when you were pregnant with me twenty-five years ago. I'm sure it was the story of the year . 'Most Beautiful Woman on the Planet Gives Birth.'"

"Stop your teasing," she scolds. "Stretch marks are nothing to joke about."

I roll my eyes at my crazy, beautiful mother. To the world, she is Lily Doyle, who some might say at one time was the most beautiful woman in the world seeing as how she was Miss America and then later crowned Miss Universe. People loved the story of how she came from the wrong side of the tracks, so-to-speak, and worked hard to earn a philanthropy degree because she wanted to help the less fortunate. She became America's Sweetheart.

"Good news, Jean Paul is in Paris this week filming some new ridiculous bit for his television show, which means I'm free all week. Let's go shopping! I'm in need of some new shoes." The excitement in my mother's voice is infectious. Jean Paul is husband number five, and from what I can tell, a very nice man, but he's always working. That seems to be okay with my mother, of course. She doesn't mind spending his money while he's away, and as much as I would love to drown in the world of Manolo, Jimmy Choo and, my personal weakness, Christian Louboutin, with her, there will be no time this weekend for that.

I sigh. "Rain check, Mother. I'm getting ready to board a flight to Vegas with Alexander King for work."

"Honey, I love you, but I absolutely don't understand you. Why on Earth do you waste that beautiful face and body that you've been blessed with on the completely dull world of business? You could've been the next big thing if you'd gotten into modeling. Out of all the things you could take from your father . . . the need to be mixed in all those suit-wearing meetings is the worst thing ever. It totally interferes with our girl time."

"I know, but I promise when I get back, we'll do something."

"Promise?" she asks. "It's been far too long, and I miss my baby girl like crazy. Your father has all your time occupied lately with this silly nonsense of invading the King Corporation."

"It's not silly, Mother. Alexander King has my future legacy in the palm of his hand. I have to find a way to stop him from taking away what will be mine someday. Staying close to him is my only option until I can figure out a way to get Buchanan Industries a deal that can save it. But I promise that as soon as I get back, we'll shop until you drop."

"Okay." She sounds satisfied with that answer. "Try to at least have a little fun while you're in Vegas. Please, don't be a stick-in-the-mud and stay in your room the entire time."

"I won't—"

"Margo, I know you. Promise me that you'll loosen up."

"Fine, but I'm sorry to say there won't be any wild stories to report when I get back."

"You are completely no fun, Margo. You have to loosen up. At least try to pretend you're twenty-five and not fifty-one like me because we both know that even I act younger than you."

I laugh. "I will try to not be a complete fun buster."

"That's my girl. Drink one for me.

"Okay. Goodbye, Mother." I laugh and hang up the phone just as the car pulls up next to King's private jet.

The driver opens my door and I take a deep breath, willing myself to put on my best bitch face and give Alexander a taste of what it's like when a woman is in charge and knows exactly what she wants.

Inside the cabin of the plane, the lone flight attendant on board greets me. Her blond hair is pulled back into a French twist on the back of her head while her bright red lipstick is a stark contrast to her porcelain skin. She has a very Gwen Stefani kind of style.

The attendant smiles at me, and I instantly relax because she appears friendly. "Good morning, Ms. Buchanan. I'm Abigail, and I'll be with you through the duration of this flight. If you need anything at all, don't hesitate to ask. Mr. King has requested that we stock the cabin with your favorite things so there's a good chance that we'll have anything that you might need."

"Um, okay. Thanks." I stumble through my answer completely dumbfounded.

This surprises me. How would Alexander King know the first thing about what I like? He doesn't really know me in the slightest and yet, somehow, he thinks he knows what my favorite things are.

I bet there's not one thing on this plane that's actually special for me. I don't know what kind of game he's playing, but I will not allow him to butter me up.

Alexander's gaze lands on me as I stride down the aisle and take the seat directly facing him instead of taking a different seat somewhere else on the private jet. He smirks at my boldness to meet him head-on and I raise my eyebrow as we stare each other down.

It's funny how we've grown accustomed to trying to one-up one another in the last week since I've begun working for him. As much as I hate to admit it, we are a lot alike. Both of us are headstrong, determined, and have this innate need to always win.

The cabin is silent for more than half the flight, and it's almost as if we're playing some weird quiet game—neither of us willing to say a word for fear that we may lose the standoff going on between us. Occasionally, he'll glance up, and I'll direct my gaze in any other direction other than at him. I mean, I'll admit, I've been checking him out. He's gorgeous, and I can't help but appreciate the view. Any woman stuck on this flight like me would do exactly the same thing. She's a liar if she tells you any different.

"Excuse me, Mr. King. Would you care for another scotch?" Abigail asks him shortly after he swallows down the last drop of amber liquid.

"Yes. That'll be fine, Abigail," he replies coolly and then gives her a polite smile which causes her to blush.

"Right away, sir." The attendant turns to me. "Are you sure I can't get you anything, Ms. Buchanan? I have Fiji water and strawberry yogurt."

I tuck a loose strand of hair behind my ear. "Wow . . . um . . ."

I hesitate. Is it simply a coincidence that Fiji just happens to be my favorite brand of water along with having my preferred flavor of yogurt?

"If you don't want those, we also have Diet Coke and Payday bars," Abigail counters.

Diet Coke I can see, but Payday bars? That's a pretty random item to keep on a plane. Especially since, judging by the looks of how fit Alexander is, he wouldn't eat such an unhealthy snack. But I guess it is possible. The man seems to drink like a fucking fish so maybe he's not all that healthy and his absurdly toned physique is just genetic.

Gah! If it is, that just gives me something else to hate him for.

I smile at Abigail as she waits patiently for me to make a selection. "I'll have a Diet Coke, please."

As soon as we're alone, Alexander's intoxicating gray eyes bore into me. "Are you not pleased with the items that I have arranged for you?"

My brow furrows. "How did you know what I like? Do you have spies watching me to ensure that I'm not digging into your business a little too much?"

He chuckles. "You act as though you still believe me to be afraid of you, Margo. I thought by now we've figured each other out. I don't seem to rattle you, and you damn sure don't affect me."

"So what's with all my favorite things on this flight?" I fire back.

He shrugs. "I'm observant. There's not much that I don't notice about the people around me, and let's just say that I've taken a very big interest in what you're up to. I like to know what makes people tick. It makes it easier for me to break them."

I stiffen my shoulders. "I've got a newsflash for you, Mr. King. I don't break."

"Everyone has their breaking point, and sooner or later, I'm going to find yours, Princess." He smirks, and I hate it when he does that. It's a sexy expression, especially on him, and I hate that I find him attractive. He is such a smug bastard. "I see the way you look at me when we argue. I turn you on even though you don't want to admit it. You and I are very similar creatures. We both love a challenge, and we both like to always be in control."

I raise my eyebrow, still not believing anything that he says. "I thought you said you didn't have spies."

He licks his plump lips slowly, causing my eyes to flick down to his mouth. "What can I say, your reputation precedes you.

Everyone knows that the Feisty Princess of Manhattan always demands her way."

My mouth gapes open. "How dare you call me that? I hate that name."

Alexander smiles. "You should learn to embrace it. A name like that means people are scared of you."

I curse the day some dumb jock in high school dubbed me that after I very colorfully turned down his eleventh attempt at asking me very bluntly to blow him. If you ask me, he deserved a punch him in the face. But sadly, the name still follows me around, even now.

I laugh bitterly. "Right. Like how you embrace yours? The Naughty King, *really?* Doesn't it bother you that half the women in this city think you're the biggest manwhore on the East Coast?"

"Not at all," he replies smoothly. "The women who call me that were fucked over by me in more ways than one, and I promise you, they fucking enjoyed every last minute of it. That's why they love to keep my name on their lips. As for the other half, they're just envious of the first."

"You are a pompous prick."

His eyes harden. "I may be, but I always do what suits me best. Women complicate the shit out of everything, and I don't have time to play their silly little games."

It's appalling how he views all women as *complications.* "Is that why you hire prostitutes? Are you really that afraid of being human and showing some compassion that you'd rather pay for sex than deal with the emotional ramifications that typically comes with it?"

"I don't see how that's any of your business, but yes. When women see me, they see a meal ticket. Why would I ever want to entertain their silly fantasies that they may be the one to make me change my ways and commit not only myself but also half of my fortune to them? No fucking way that's ever going to happen."

I roll my eyes. "Not all women think that way."

"Are you telling me that you don't?"

"No," I answer automatically. "My family is already wealthy. Why would I need to marry for money?"

"For the same reason a lot of women do. Soon, I'll be taking your father's company. How long do you think it'll take before your family's fortune runs out? Doesn't that scare you?"

"No," I repeat. "That's not going to happen. My father—"

"Yes, it will. Neither of you can stop the inevitable from happening. The contacts we're meeting in Vegas are long-time business associates of mine, and there's nothing you'll be able to do to steal them away from me, which is why it doesn't bother me to bring you along."

I open my mouth to fire back in my defense, but he keeps going, cutting me off.

"Honestly, if I were you, Margo, I would probably just quit now and work on finding a wealthy schmuck to marry. You've got a nice ass and decent sized tits, so I'm sure you won't have a problem securing a cushy future as long as you don't mind fucking some old, ugly motherfucker."

I grip the armrest of my seat and dig my nails into the cream-colored leather. It takes everything in me to not jump up and smack the ever-living shit out of this man.

I take a deep breath and count to five in my head before I blow the air out slowly through my nose. This helps me refocus and not fall into the little game he's playing with me.

I swallow hard. "I'll keep that in mind, but I would much rather spend my time figuring out ways to take you down."

"Suit yourself. But I'm warning you, Ms. Buchanan, I don't play fair." There's a wicked gleam in his eye, and there's no telling what he's planning to do to torture me, but I have to be ready for any move he tries to make.

My father is counting on me to figure out a way to save his company and my family's future.

Chapter VII PROVOCATEUR

Alexander

No matter the time of day, the lights in Las Vegas are always putting on a show. The limo pulls up to the Hard Rock Casino, and I glance over at Margo as the driver stops the car.

She hasn't said much to me since our heated little discussion. Every time we talk, I seem to piss her off, which is exactly what I want to do. I want to become the itch festering under her skin that she's dying to scratch. The more she hates me—the more she'll think about me and how much she can't wait to be rid of me.

So why do I feel like a bastard and have this urge to apologize?

I shake my head to purge myself of the crazy thought. I need her out of my fucking hair. Her presence distracts me, and that's not good. I need a clear head for business. This weekend is going to be pure torture.

The minute the driver opens the door, I step out and then turn with my hand out to assist Margo. My eyes dart down to her sexy long legs, and I wonder if she knows how much she turns me on with those damn skirts she flits around in all the time. I wonder if she does it intentionally to drive me out of my fucking mind. The whole naughty businesswoman look she has going on works well for her. Even when she wears those little black-rimmed glasses, she's still hot as hell.

We're immediately greeted by a short, pudgy man wearing a black suit with his black hair slicked back like he's a 1940s mobster. "Good afternoon, Mr. King. My name is Coleman, and I'll be your personal concierge during your stay. Allow me to escort you to your room." After a quick snap of his fingers, two bellhops rush to the back of the car to retrieve our luggage before following us into the hotel.

The elevator doors ding before opening, and I stop myself from placing my hand on the small of Margo's back. I cannot allow myself to touch her because whenever I do, strange things happen to me. The last time we touched was in my office when she grabbed my cock and told me that I was the one who was fucked. She rattled me. I hadn't expected her to do that so it threw me off for a brief moment. But now that I know what she's capable of, I won't allow her to ever gain the upper hand again. I have to be careful and keep her at a distance.

Silence surrounds us once we're shut inside the tiny space and begin ascending, but it's not awkward. Either Margo and I are doing our best to ignore one another or we're at each other's throats. There isn't any middle ground between us where we can just be casual. Diem's right. We can't go on like this. I need to work on being friendlier. Having her favorite things on the plane was a small start, but I'm going to have to step it up a notch and dial my personality down a bit. The last thing I need is to fight with this woman in Yamada's presence. He'd have a fucking field day with that shit. I don't need him thinking that she has the upper hand in this situation.

The elevator dings and Coleman smiles. "Ah, here we are. Right this way to the Provocateur Suite."

Margo's shoulders stiffen as she halts in her tracks. "What happened to the Paradise Tower Penthouse that I booked?"

Coleman frowns. "We emailed you earlier this morning to notify you that the Paradise Penthouse would be unavailable for your stay this weekend. Our last guests . . . well, let's just say they put the room out of commission for a bit. It's in desperate need of repairs, and since this was a last-minute booking, I'm afraid the only penthouse that we have available for your duration is the Provocateur Suite."

Margo shakes her head, causing her black curls to bounce around. "You can't honestly expect me to stay there with my boss. I didn't mind sharing a traditional penthouse, but this is unacceptable."

"I'm sorry, Ms. Buchanan. Like we explained on the phone at the time of your reservation, this weekend we have several major events and conventions, and we are completely booked."

Margo sighs and her shoulders slump. "Okay. Since I really don't have a choice in the matter, but—" she swings around and points her gaze directly at me "—I expect you to remain professional."

I hold up my hands in surrender. "I don't have the slightest idea of what you mean. It's a room for Christ's sake, Margo."

"It's not just *any* room. It's the sex slave suite," she whispers harshly.

My eyebrows jerk up in surprise. I was definitely not expecting this curveball. "This room is right down your twisted little path, but I swear to God if you spend the weekend tying up random women in a place that we have to share, you might not leave with your balls intact," she fires at me.

A grin spreads across my face. Her spunk is absolutely the hottest fucking thing I've seen in a long time. "Margo, the only woman I plan on tying up this weekend is you."

I know I just said I shouldn't touch her, but I don't think that's going to be possible. Especially not while being reminded of sex every time I turn around in the room we're sharing. She's too damn sexy, and I won't be able to resist the temptation.

Margo's nostrils flare. "Don't count on it, King."

We stand there staring each other down. Both of us determined to be the one who comes out the victor this weekend.

Coleman clears his throat next to us. "Okay, then, why don't I show you to the suite?"

I roll my shoulders and straighten my tie but never take my eyes off Margo. "Lead the way, Coleman."

"Right away, Mr. King. This way."

We follow behind him in silence. This woman knows how to push my buttons like no other. If I'm being honest, I like that she challenges me. I've never had a woman do that before, and in an odd way, it's refreshing. She's not like all the other fucking doormats who typically surround me and do whatever I say just because of who I am.

The moment the door opens, I can tell that this is unlike any other penthouse I've been in before, and that's saying a lot considering how much I travel. The walls are deep red while masculine black leather furniture fills the space. A large stocked bar with all the top-shelf liquor one could ever desire sits near the entrance.

To the left, Coleman walks us over to one of the master suites, which is a room with three queen-sized beds pushed together complete with holograms of women writhing on the bed. This is indeed a place where sexual fantasies are meant to be explored.

We pass back through the living room area into another room that contains a padded exam table like you see at a doctor's office, but there are steel hoops bolted to it. Obviously, this table is intended to have people tied to it. One black tiled wall has more steel hoops attached to it, and there's a steel birdcage that's big enough to fit an adult into that sits in the corner. Next to the cage is a large wooden 'X' that's attached to the wall with loops made for tying someone to. A tall, black bookcase sits on the opposite wall. A couple of boxes that are clearly vibrators, sexual lotions, whips and every other thing you can think of to use in a fuck room fills the shelves.

"This room is another part of what makes this suite so special. It's fully equipped and has sexual enhancers that will increase the enjoyment. Any items that you do choose to use will be discreetly added to your bill. Attached you will find the second master suite—" Coleman motions toward the bedroom, but I can no longer concentrate on what he's saying.

All I can think about is how much I want to tie Margo to this table and explore every inch of her body. Having this man in here with us is a distraction to what I really want to know.

"Leave us," I order Coleman.

He bows his head. "As you wish."

As he opens the door, he instructs the bellhops to leave our luggage at the entrance before they all exit without another word.

I turn my focus back to Margo. Her wide eyes tell me that even though she won't admit it, being alone in this room with me scares her. She feels this weird sexual connection between us too. I know she does. She just won't give in and admit it. If we'd just fuck, I'm sure all this weird tension would disappear and we could both focus on what we actually came out here to do.

I swallow hard and then glance at the two master suite doors that are on the opposite sides of this fantasy room.

I motion from one room to the other. "Lady's choice."

"That's gracious of you considering that's not how you typically operate. By the way it looked in your office the other day, it seemed like it was all about your choices first," she mutters as she turns away from me toward the room that we hadn't toured yet.

Before I realize it, I'm snatching her wrist, stopping her mid-step and forcing her to look at me. "How do you know that when I'm with a woman I'm *not* paying for that I don't put her first?"

She raises one eyebrow. "You're too much of a selfish prick to put anyone's needs before your own."

My pulse thunders beneath my skin. "Maybe I need to change your perception of me then—show you just how giving I can be when I want to. This suite—it's the perfect place for us to fuck and get it out of our systems. Don't you agree? Just imagine all the ways I could make you come while I have you strapped to that table."

I can't deny that just being in here and seeing all the props has me picturing what it would be like to tie her up and spank her ass before feeling her pussy wrapped around my cock.

Her head falls back slightly as she lets out a low sarcastic laugh. "I would never fuck you. You are *not* my type."

I lick my lips as I close the distance between us until her chest presses against me. "A man with a big cock who knows how to use it is *every* woman's type, and believe me, baby, I'm the best fuck you'll ever have."

I can no longer hold back. The sweet smell of her perfume and the very essence of her surround me and the need to have her—possess her—consumes me. My hands wrap around her waist and then slide down her perfect ass to find the hem of her skirt. The tips of my fingers graze the bare flesh on her legs.

Her entire body shivers, but she never takes her eyes off me as she takes a deep breath. "Prove it."

She doesn't have to tell me twice. I seize the opportunity and slide my hand up her back so I could tangle my fingers into her hair. I slam my mouth against hers with so much need it's almost overwhelming. Her lips part, allowing enough room for my tongue to snake into her mouth, and she moans.

I'm such a fucking goner.

She tastes like heaven, and I'm too much of a sinner to resist devouring every inch of her. Tonight, I will own her body. Tonight, I will make her mine.

Chapter IX FALLING

Margo

He's taking what he wants without apologies, and it's so damn hot.

His hands are everywhere: in my hair, on my ass, cupping my face while he deepens our kiss. Alexander King definitely knows how to touch a woman and set her skin on fire. When his lips attack mine, I throw my hands in his hair to try to immerse myself in him. Alexander wraps his arms around me, tugging me closer while never breaking our kiss.

He grabs the material at the bottom of my tucked in blouse and pulls the fabric free of my pencil skirt. One by one, he pops the buttons open with his skilled hands and when he frees the last one, he slides the material off my shoulders, allowing his fingers to trace my bare skin before my shirt falls to the floor. The hem of my skirt creeps up my thighs as Alexander slides it to get better access.

He presses himself against me. The roughness of his trousers against me causes a tingle to erupt all over my body. My panties grow instantly wet as he presses against the sensitive flesh between my legs while unzipping my skirt, loosening it so it falls in a pool around my ankles.

I stand there in nothing but my red, satin lingerie and black Jimmy Choos before him. He steps back, appraising me from head to toe with hungry eyes. I should feel self-conscious about him staring at me like this, but I don't. He makes me feel wanted and powerful by staring at me like I'm the most mouthwatering thing he's ever seen.

Alexander licks his lips and then drags his teeth slowly over his bottom lip as he closes the distance between us.

His toned body presses into me, and he grips my hips, yanking my pelvis against his and allowing me to feel his erection through his slacks. "You are the sexiest fucking thing I've ever seen. I'm going to enjoy this, and I promise you will too if you give yourself over to me completely."

Before I can say anything else, he crushes his lips to mine, plunging his tongue inside my mouth, and making my knees go a little weak from the sheer intensity of it. An ache builds between my legs, and I realize that I've never been this turned on in my life. There's no way I can put a stop to this now. I need him inside me too damn much.

My fingers snake into his hair, and I love the fact that he has just enough length for me to grab onto.

Strong hands slide down my ass and then cup the back side of my thighs. My legs wrap around his waist as he hoists me up with ease. He walks toward the table in the middle of the room and sets me down, pressing himself firmly between my legs.

I writhe against him and the soft material of his slacks allows his hard cock to rub against my most sensitive flesh. My entire body craves the relief only he can bring me. The smoothness of his well-manicured hands moving across my skin causes goosebumps to erupt over every inch of me. My breasts ache as he moves around to my back and unhooks my bra, freeing them for his pleasure. A warm trail of kisses leave fire in their wake as he works his way down my neck, nipping, teasing and promising passion as he moves past my collarbone. He takes one of my nipples into his mouth and I suck a rush of air through my clenched teeth.

Alexander opens his mouth and sticks his tongue out as I watch him swirl it around the taut pink flesh. I wrap my legs around him tighter and work my pelvis up and down.

This man has me so ready.

"You want this as much as I do." His hooded eyes flick up in my direction. "This is going to be fun."

He bends down and reaches for something under the table. The rattle of chains startles me. I guess I hadn't noticed them under there during the tour, but to be honest I was so uncomfortable standing in this room with Alexander that I didn't pay much attention to the small details. Before I know what's going on, he wraps a cuff around one of my wrists and then quickly follows with another shackle.

I furrow my brow. "What the . . . ?"

Alexander's face lights up with a wicked grin. "It's time to play."

My eyes widen as he locks my other arm into place as well. "You're tying me up?"

He nods and pushes me back with a firm hand, forcing me back on my elbows. "I want control."

Alexander's fingers find the wet spot on my underwear. "Mmmm. So wet. That's fucking sexy. I don't think I've ever wanted to taste something so badly."

"I . . ." My mouth hangs open, unable to complete a coherent thought as he grabs the silky material on my hips and rips it with ease before he tosses the scraps of satin that were once my panties to the floor.

I bite my lip as I sit on the table before him completely exposed for his viewing pleasure. His gray eyes slowly trail over every inch of me, taking his time to appreciate the view.

He pushes my knees apart again as he slides between them and then teases my top lip with his tongue. "Do you want me to touch you?"

His hand slithers up my thigh, and for the first time in my life, I'm at a loss for words. I squeeze my eyes shut, still fighting against giving him possession of me, as he wants. I'm all for having sex, but him taking complete control . . . well, that's just not my style.

"Beg," he commands. "Beg for it like a good girl, and maybe . . . *just* maybe, I'll give you what you want."

The man is infuriating. I'm finally giving in and allowing him to ravage my body and now he wants me to beg? Get fucking real.

"No," I say with authority in my voice.

"No?" His warm breath tickles my cheek as he breathes against my neck. "I need to hear you plead, Margo. If you want to come, then you need to say *please.*"

His finger slides slowly against my clit and my entire body trembles. I hate the way every inch of me aches for him—craves his stupid, electrifying touch.

"Fuck you," I whisper, trying my best to keep it together and stay strong as I teeter on the edge of an orgasm. "I beg for no man."

"You'll beg for me, Margo. I can promise you that." He kisses a warm trail down my neck as he continues to work my clit at a frustratingly slow pace. "I can keep this up all night. How long do you think it'll be before you concede and I'm fucking you senseless right here on this very table? Hmmm?"

He pushes his thick finger inside me, causing me to moan. "Oh, God."

"Tell me how much you need me to fuck you. Beg, Margo. Let me own you."

He works his finger in and out, curving up at just the right spot each time to cause my entire body to tingle. I throw my head back and moan as I rub against the heel of his hand.

"Such a greedy girl." He teasingly nips my shoulder before whispering, "You know what I want to hear. Say it and I'll give you what you want."

My brain keeps telling me that I should fight him—that giving into him will show weakness—but my stupid body is all too willing and ready. I want him. I want him to do all the things he's promising to me. I want him to make me feel good.

His thumb flicks over my clit, and I whimper.

Oh. My. God. This is more than I can handle. How in the hell am I supposed to resist him when he has me teetering on the edge so quickly?

"I'm waiting, Margo," he growls.

His demanding words cause me to shiver, and combined with how damn good he's making me feel with his hand, I'm willing to do just about anything he asks in the heat of the moment.

I snap my eyes open and bite my lip. "Please."

"Please, *what?*" he probes as he circles his thumb around my throbbing nub.

"Fuck me, please. Make me come." The begging tone of my voice appalls me, but I know that my brain has completely allowed my body to take control here. Desire clouds me to the point that I can barely think straight, let alone worry about how embarrassed I should be for begging this man for what I want.

"Good girl." Alexander bites his lip as he brings his hands up to cup my face so he can gaze deep into my eyes. "I've wanted to taste you ever since you stepped foot into my office."

His words make me shiver again with excitement.

He lightly kisses my lips. "I'm going to make you come so hard that you won't even remember your own name."

Alexander steps back and begins unbuttoning his shirt, and my fingers itch to help push it open so I can see his body, but my wrists remain shackled, limiting my movement. If I'm being honest, I've imagined what he'd look like naked more than a few hundred times. I bite my lip as his perfectly sculpted abs come into view when he drops his white dress shirt onto the floor.

Holy Mary mother of Joseph! Alexander's body is better than I imagined in my wildest dreams. His chest definition exceeds that of the most lickable men in magazines, not to mention he has biceps that last for days and the sexy 'V' cut into his hips that dips down into his pants.

I think I'm about to lose my mind. Can this man be any hotter?

He smirks when I don't take my eyes off him. "Just think . . . you haven't even seen the best part of me yet."

This man is absolutely wicked and entirely too sexy for his own good. He's the perfect example of a man who knows what he's blessed with and isn't afraid to be cocky about it. Confidence is such a turn on.

Almost like a strip tease, he unzips his pants and then shoves them down, along with his boxer-briefs, leaving them in a pile on the floor. My eyes widen at the sight of his completely naked body. He wasn't kidding when he said that he had a big cock. I'm not one who typically refers to a man's appendage as beautiful, but that's exactly what Alexander King's penis is. It stands proud in all its silky glory, and my fingers ache to touch it.

King turns to the cabinet and grabs a condom before opening a package containing a small silver bullet vibrator. After testing to make sure the vibrator works, he stalks toward me with both items. "There are a lot of toys in there. Do you think we should try them all?"

The thought of my body as his playground long enough to test out everything on those shelves causes me to shudder. I don't think I'll be able to handle it. I'm nearly ready to combust, and he's barely touched me. There's no way I'd survive.

Alexander sets the condom down and then presses his lips to mine. "Relax, Margo. Tonight's all about you. I won't do anything you don't want me to. You can tell me to stop anytime you'd like."

I want to scream out for him just to touch me again. No one has ever left me teetering on the verge of an orgasm for so long before. This man is about to drive me insane.

His tongue seeks entrance into my mouth, and I melt into him. "Spread your legs." I do exactly what he asks and watch as he kisses a trail down my body, throwing my legs over both shoulders as he drops to his knees. He grabs my ass, yanking my pussy closer to his mouth.

His tongue flicking across my clit sends an electric surge through me and I hiss. "Jesus."

"No, baby, it's just me," he murmurs before he pushes a finger inside me and licks my slick folds. "Mmmm. You taste just as delicious as I expected."

Alexander continues to work me into a frenzy, and the urge to reach out and grab a handful of his thick hair to hold him against me is strong, but my bound arms won't allow it. The heat of his tongue against my throbbing clit is almost more than I can handle. All I can do is lie on this table, exposed, and wait on his mercy. Only he can give me the pleasure that I desire to calm this ache building inside me.

The sound of the vibrator echoes around the room. Relief floods me because I know the moment he touches my clit with it, I'll finally be able to come. I hold my breath as he traces the outside of my lips with it, but he's careful to steer clear of where I need the sensation the most.

My head drops back as he kisses the inside of my thigh. I need him in me, filling me, to cure this burning desire that's rocking me to the core.

"Alexander . . ." His name comes out in a breathy whisper, as he presses the vibrator into my entrance. "I'm so close. Please."

"Told you that you'd beg." His gray eyes look up at me, and I can tell he's smiling, but it's impossible for me to fire back a snarky comment. The next thing I know, he's licking and sucking my clit like it's his only job in the world while he continues to use the toy.

My pussy has never been this stimulated, and it's pushing me to the edge already.

"Oh. My God. That's it. Keep going," I plead.

Both legs resting on his shoulders begin shaking uncontrollably and an intense tingle erupts in my core and then spreads over every inch of my body. I squeeze my eyes shut and I swear to God that I see fireworks as I come hard just like he promised. My entire body jerks as I scream out his name, but he keeps going, prolonging my pleasure to the point that it feels so good that it actually hurts.

Just when I don't think I can take another second, he stops his delicious torture and stands as he switches off the vibrator.

With quick movements, he releases both of my wrists from the shackles before pulling them one at a time to his mouth. He inhales deeply like he's trying to commit my scent to memory as he presses soft kisses to my flesh.

He stares down at me with a grin. "I love seeing that satisfied look on your face but don't get too comfortable. We're just getting started."

Oh, my.

My heart flutters with anticipation. If this was just the appetizer, dinner might damn near kill me.

He threads his fingers into my hair and pulls me into a deep kiss, allowing me to taste myself on him. This kiss makes me feel so desired that, for a moment, I can't imagine why I refused his advances. I should've allowed this to happen from the first moment he offered to fuck me.

He pulls back and stares into my eyes. "Stay."

The warning that flashes in his eyes tells me that disobeying his command is not an option. I still need him like crazy so I don't even debate not doing as he says.

I find myself biting my lip as I stare after Alexander as he makes his way back over to the toy shelf. His ass is divine. It's round with just the right amount of bubble, and I just want to get my hands on it. Some women are all about the arms, others the backs, but my weakness is a toned male booty. Alexander's is so tight that I bet you could bounce quarters off that thing.

My eyes roam over the well-defined muscles of his back as they stretch and move while he pokes around at all the other items on the shelf.

There's a glimmer in his gray eyes as he turns to me with a blindfold in one hand and a riding crop in the other.

I shake my head as he begins to stalk toward me. "No. You are not tying me up and spanking me. That's so fucking cliché."

That cocky smirk returns, making him even more fucking attractive. "How can millions of people be wrong about the enjoyment of the combination?"

I fold my arms. "What some people find pleasurable is just wrong then."

"How do you know that's true? I bet you've never even tried it." He raises one eyebrow in challenge.

"I . . ." I what? There's no defense here, considering he's right. Dammit, I hate that.

Alexander smiles. "Thought so. Off the table."

"Alexander . . ."

"Off the table." The authority in his voice rings around the small room.

He's so damn bossy. If I still weren't horny as hell, I would tell him to go take a flying fucking leap, but seeing as how I've come this far, I might as well play along.

My pride has already been tossed out the window. What else do I have to lose?

I hop off the table and train my eyes on Alexander as he closes the distance between us. "What now?"

"Close your eyes." With gentle hands, he covers my eyes with the black mask. "I've always heard that if you take away one sense that it will heighten the others. Let's test that theory, shall we?"

The warmth of his hands sliding down my body causes my mouth to drift open. The tease of his skin on mine has my body in overdrive. When his hands grip my hips, he spins me around and bends me over the table that I was just chained to.

"Grab the other side of the table and don't you dare let go."

A lump in my throat builds as the image of the crop flashes in my brain. This man is about to spank my bare ass. I should stop this—tell him this isn't happening—but I can't bring myself to do it.

While the logical part of my brain is screaming at me to end this and stand my ground and remember that Alexander King is the enemy, another part is squealing with delight as it awaits the delicious torture that he's about to inflict.

Before I have too much time to think about it, the distinct snap of something being hit sounds, and almost instantly, there's a small tingle on my right butt cheek.

"Hurt?" he asks with an inflection in his voice that implies his curiosity.

"No," I answer honestly. "But—"

He doesn't give me time to further protest. The second swat comes just as unexpected as the first.

"Ah . . ." A cry slips from my lips. It isn't one of pain, but of pleasure, and that surprises me.

Stupid traitorous body. I can't believe it's actually enjoying this.

"You liked that one, didn't you? Another?"

No.

"Yes!" I hiss.

My stupid body has completely taken over now.

Smack.

Then comes the sweet burn that follows just like the last two times, only this time was a little harder.

I toss my head back and moan.

Smack.

This one wakes me up as pain sears through me.

"Ah. Shit. That hurt." I yank off the blindfold and spin around to face him. "We're done."

Alexander shakes his head and then presses against me. "We are so far from done, Margo. You are my greatest challenge—one I'm determined to conquer."

"You—" I start to tell him this is over, but at that very second, he rakes his teeth over his bottom lip, and all I can think about is having that mouth on me again.

Without invitation, I throw my arms around him and attack him with my lips. There's no resistance from him because suddenly Alexander's hands are everywhere, tracing, teasing, and exploring every inch of me. It's like he can't get enough of me and I love the way that he makes me feel.

I'd be lying to myself if I say I haven't wanted this with him since the first time he threatened to fuck me. No man has ever aroused me this much. His take-charge attitude draws me in. It's animalistic and sexy—a complete turn-on.

Alexander King is hard to resist.

"You don't know how hard it was for me to be patient. I feel like I've waited a lifetime to have you just like this. I've even had dreams about tasting you," he growls. "You're exactly my favorite type of woman, and I can't wait to get my cock deep in that sweet pussy of yours."

His naughty words make my blood pump even faster.

He slides his hand between us and flicks my still throbbing clit. "Alexander . . ." I say his name almost like a whisper.

"Do you want me inside you?"

I throw my head back and moan as he continues to tease me. "Yesssss!"

"Then tell me, baby. I want to hear some naughty words come out of that beautiful mouth."

"I . . ." I pause. God, I so want this. I just hate the fact that he's asking me to beg, and what's worse is that I'm so turned on by him that I'd just about say anything he damn near wants. I need the relief that only he can bring me.

Alexander licks my top lip. "Say it, Margo."

I close my eyes but quickly reopen them so he knows I mean what I say. "Fuck me.

A devilish smile creeps onto his face. "I knew you were a naughty girl deep down."

He kneads my breasts while rubbing the tip of his cock against my clit as he continues to study my face. He reaches for the condom, and I seize the opportunity to wrap my hand around his cock and stroke him while he opens the wrapper.

He licks his lips and watches me work him. "Your hands on me feel so good." He hands me the thin piece of rubber. "You do it since you're so good with your hands."

I pinch the tip as I roll it down his thick cock. Pure lust fills Alexander's gray eyes are they roam over my naked body. His mouth drifts open when I spread my legs wider for him.

This man has me completely turned on, and I'm doing things that I normally wouldn't do.

"I'm such a fucking bastard for taking you like this. It's not right considering our situation, but I can't seem to stop myself. You are a very desirable woman, Margo Buchanan." Alexander leans down and kisses me again.

My toes curl inside my stilettos as I wrap my legs around his waist, pushing him toward my entrance. "I'd be lying if I said I didn't want you too."

A low growl emits from his throat as he penetrates me with the head of his cock. "Holy fuck! I wasn't expecting you to be so fucking tight. Amazing."

I slide my hand up his back. "I won't break. I don't want you to be gentle. I want you to fuck me and make it count."

Alexander bites my bottom lip and pushes his shaft inside of me all the way down to the base. He pulls back and then slides into me again.

I whimper wanting him to move faster inside me.

"Patience, baby. You feel so fucking good. If I don't go slowly this will be over before either of us is ready."

He grabs my waist and picks up the pace, pumping into me faster and harder. Sweat slicks his back as the slapping of our skin echoes around the room. I stare up at his face, surprised to find his gaze on mine. It's like he's trying to commit my face to memory as he fucks my brains out.

"Mmmm yeah. So fucking perfect. Sweetest pussy I've ever had." The words tumble from his lips and knowing that he's feeling just as good as I am causes another orgasm to rip through me.

"Alexander!" I cry as he works me into a frenzy.

"Oh. Oh. I'm coming. Oh, God," I moan as my body erupts in complete euphoria.

His movements become more rigid and intense as he works hard to find his own release.

"Goddamn, baby. Shit," he says before he growls as a shudder tears through him as he comes hard.

He buries his head in the crook of my neck. Both of us still breathing hard and he's still buried deep. "That was . . . fuck, that was amazing."

I smile as I twirl a wild strand of hair poking out from his head. "I agree."

Alexander raises his head and looks me in the eye. "I don't know how in the hell I'm supposed to remain strictly professional with you now. You're fucking addictive. I already want to do that again."

I close my eyes as the realization of what just happened between us hits. "This is going to complicate the hell out of things."

He nods. "Yes, but we're going to have to find a way to figure things out and coexist. We still have a business deal to get through."

The reminder of why we're actually here is like a splash of cold water on the face. No matter how amazing sex with Alexander King is, it can never happen again.

Chapter X
MR. YAMADA

Margo

I study myself in the mirror of this ridiculous hotel suite and wonder if anyone can tell that this is the face of a woman who just fucked her boss?

Shit.

I'm not sure what in the hell just came over me. One minute I was in the hallway completely composed and fending off his advances, and then the next thing I know we're kissing and I instigated his advances.

The moment he put his hands on me in the sex room, I lost it. They were so strong, so sure and felt too damn good. It was amazing for once to have a man who wasn't afraid to take control and pull me outside my rigid box. I would've never allowed a man to do the things that he did to me—restraints—but Alexander's forwardness and sex appeal got to me. I gave in during a moment of weakness and became just another easy lay for him, giving him full control. I've never experienced that, and if I'm being honest, it was very liberating.

I just hate that it was Alexander King. He's supposed to be my mortal enemy. Not the man who opened me up to exploration and a sexual revolution.

What in the hell am I going to do now?

A knock on the door startles me out of my thoughts. "Margo? Are you ready?"

I smooth my hair away from my face but don't dare open the door. I'm not ready to face Alexander just yet. "For what?"

"It's nearly two. I'm scheduled to meet with my contact at the pool. I'll wait for you if you're nearly finished getting ready," he says, and it instantly causes my shoulders to slump.

I stare down at my still nude body wrapped in a fluffy white hotel towel. "Go ahead without me. I'll be down in a bit."

"Margo . . ." There's hesitation in his voice. "Are you okay? You sound off."

I don't answer because I can't find the right words to express the things going through my mind. On one hand, I'm feeling amazing because I've just had the most mind-blowing sexual experience, but on the other, I'm completely torn in a way I didn't expect. Sadness for the loss of something that I know will never happen again. Being with Alexander had to be a one-time thing. It can never happen again. Sleeping with him was never part of the plan. I don't do random sex. My heart gets too invested, and I refuse to be just another notch in Alexander King's insanely long bedpost.

"Margo?" When I still don't bother to answer, the handle of the bathroom door rotates just before it swings open, revealing a shirtless Alexander wearing a pair of black swimming trunks.

"I didn't say that you could come in here," I scold him and then tighten the towel around me.

He tilts his head, and his gorgeous gray eyes bore into me. "I thought we were long past formalities at this point."

A shiver shoots down my spine. "Just because we've seen each other naked and . . ."

He lifts his eyebrows and finishes my sentence for me. "Fucked?"

I straighten my shoulders. "Yes. That. It doesn't mean that it's going to happen again or that things are suddenly different between us."

Alexander pulls his plump, bitable lips into a tight line. "So you want to just forget it ever happened and go right back to hating each other?"

I nod. "That's exactly what I want."

He lets out an exasperated sigh before running his hand down the back of his neck. "Fine. Then get your ass ready and get down to the pool. We have business to attend to."

I flinch at the sudden change in the tone of his voice, but I like that he's in agreement and doing exactly as I ask. When I open my mouth to tell him to fuck off and that I'd be down when I'm good and ready, I quickly close it when I see a flash of pain in his eyes before he turns and walks out of the bathroom.

I sigh the moment I hear the door slam when he leaves the suite.

This situation is all kinds of fucked up.

After getting myself together after a quick shower, I make my way down to the pool party that the Hard Rock calls Rehab. The scene before me causes me to raise my eyebrows. This place is something straight out of the Spring Break handbook. There are bodies everywhere—all of them dancing to the techno beat spun by the DJ.

This is seriously where King is meeting a business contact? Good luck talking business out here.

When I get through security, I merge into the crowd. Several pairs of hungry male eyes watch me intently as I pass by, and suddenly I wish I would've let Alexander wait on me. I don't like feeling like a piece of meat on display.

One dark-haired man with a set of toned abs and wide smile grabs my wrist as I pass by. "Damn! You've got the nicest set of tits I've seen all day."

I fight the urge to smack him in the face because I know that technically I'm out here for business purposes and getting arrested for assault wouldn't be a good look.

"Not interested." I attempt to twist out of his grasp, but there's no such luck.

The man tightens his hold and attempts to jerk me against his chest. "Let me feel those titties on me."

"Get off me!" I shove my arms between us and push with all my might, but he's too big and I can't force him off.

"Play nice, baby," he says, and the distinct smell of beer wafts into my face.

Before I have a chance to say anything else, the man flies back and Alexander steps between us. Alexander's hands ball into fists at his side as his entire body tenses.

"If you know what's good for you, you'll walk away. Now." The low growl in Alexander's voice emits such a warning that the man instantly throws his hands up in surrender and backs away without another word.

Alexander stands still, shielding me until he's sure the man is gone, and I have to admit that I'm grateful for his presence.

He slowly turns toward me. "You all right?"

I nod. "Yes. Thank you for that. I don't know what I would've done if you hadn't been here."

"Don't worry, Margo. Nobody will dare touch you while I'm around."

His confident words cause butterflies to erupt in my belly. It makes me feel safe knowing that he's looking out for me.

"Oh, shit. Did you see that?" The voice comes from a small Asian man who looks like he's straight out of a rap video with his gold chains and baseball cap. He slaps Alexander's shoulder and laughs. "Dat madafucka just got punked. I think he shit his pants. He better not come back for seconds because Yamada might just have to step in and he doesn't want any of this."

Alexander rolls his eyes and then turns toward the man. "Next time he's all yours, big guy."

The man turns toward me and lowers the gold-rimmed sunglasses down the bridge of his nose. His dark eyes drink me in from head to toe before he flicks his gaze in Alexander's direction. "Are you with dis fine piece?"

Alexander sighs. "Yamada, this is Margo Buchanan. She's my assistant."

"I bet." Yamada laughs and then pushes his glasses back over his eyes. "Just like old times, King. You bring all the fly honeys to the party."

That takes me back. Old times? It sounds like Alexander's relationship with Yamada goes far beyond a business one. How in the hell am I supposed to possibly find a way to infiltrate their business relationship if they are as good of friends as they seem to be?

"Don't look so serious, Dime Piece," Yamada says to me. "This is a party. Lighten up. We need to dance."

My mouth gapes open as I look at Alexander, but he's no help. He simply shrugs. "There's no stopping him when he's on a mission to party. Just go with it."

Yamada grabs my hand. "Come with Yamada. I'll show you a good time."

I glance back at Alexander while this odd little man leads me along, and he just simply grins and waves before the crowd swallows him up.

"Why do you keep referring to yourself in the third person?" I complain as he weaves us through the crowd.

He turns toward me, pulling the sunglasses down the bridge of his nose and peering at me over the top of them again with an expression that I can only describe as dumbfounded. "Because that's what all the badass madafakas do."

For a split second, I don't know if he's actually serious or not, but when he winks at me, I can't hold back a chuckle.

Yamada smiles, clearly pleased with my lightened mood, and then pushes his sunglasses back up. "Now that's a killer smile. Let's go shake it so I can show off that the hottest chick in this place is grinding on me."

This man was so not what I was expecting when I imagined coming out here to meet Alexander's business contact. I guess what I expected was a man that was, well, something more along the lines of my father—an accomplished older man. Instead, I get a younger guy who's busy twerking in front of me at a crowded pool party.

I'm not sure I can take this guy seriously when it comes to anything business related, but he seems to be a damn good time. I'm going to have to rethink how I'm going to get in good with this man. For now, I'm going to dance because that seems like what he wants to do.

Yamada pops up and faces me. "Now that we're alone, we can talk."

I'm still dancing in time to the beat when I ask, "About what?"

"How long you know King?"

"Not long, but I've always known of him. Manhattan isn't as big of a place as people think." I tuck a loose strand of my dark hair behind my ear and figure this is my chance to get a little information too. "You two seem close. How did you meet?"

"In college," he answers before doing a spin. "I met him when I came to America to study. He was floored by my awesomeness, and we've been friends ever since."

"Wow," I say, honestly surprised. "That's cool that you two have stayed in touch."

He shrugs. "When Yamada makes a friend, it's for life, and now we're business partners."

We dance for a few more beats before he asks, "You fuck him yet, or does Yamada still have a shot?"

My mouth drops open and my eyes widen.

"Aw, shit. You did. I can tell by the look on your face. That's okay, you're only the second woman King has ever been able to beat Yamada to."

That piques my curiosity. "Who was the other?"

"Jess," Yamada answers. "His girlfriend from college. You know, the bitch who screwed him over and broke his heart."

I raise my eyebrows. "I didn't think he had one of those."

Yamada tilts his head. "What? A heart?"

I nod and keep dancing with him.

He shakes his head in response. "You obviously don't know him then, because he has one of the biggest hearts I've ever seen. I call him a pussy all the time for wearing it on his sleeve like a bitch. He needs to toughen up."

Little does Yamada know, Alexander King has done an excellent job of making me, along with most of the women on the Upper East Side, believe that he's a ruthless prick. I think I know him a little better than Yamada at this point.

"I think he's plenty tough. Matter of fact, I think he's a pompous ass," I admit.

Yamada throws his head back in a fit of laughter. "I like you. You and Yamada will get along just fine."

I glance over at Alexander, who has found a seat at one of the bars. It's like I can feel his eyes on me, studying every move I make. I'm positive that pushing him away like I did earlier was the best choice for my sanity, not to mention my heart, but it doesn't stop my stupid body from being drawn to him. It's going to be a lot harder to ignore his advances now, especially since I know what it's like to be with him. It'll be difficult to turn down those intense promises of pleasure because he does a damn fine job of delivering.

I spend the rest of the afternoon dancing and drinking with Yamada, while my brain works on trying to figure out the complex puzzle that is Alexander King—a puzzle that according to Yamada, I don't have the first fucking clue about.

Chapter XI
ROUND TWO

Alexander

I lay in the middle bed of this crazy room, trying to relax. I haven't even had the energy to change out of my board shorts or throw on a shirt. Hanging out at Rehab all day and watching Margo while she pretended I didn't exist, was fucking brutal. The image of her spread out before me, moaning my name in ecstasy while she came stayed in the forefront of my mind. All I could think about was how much I wanted to experience that again. How I wanted to fuck her again. How I wanted my name on her lips as she loses all control.

It makes me hard right now just thinking about it.

But Margo wouldn't so much as give me the time of day. Instead, she spent the afternoon laughing at every joke Yamada told and ignored me. Even when I asked her a direct question, all I received were short one-word answers.

It sucks knowing the fact that I'll probably never have her again, which is completely fucked up considering who I am. I'm Alexander King. I'm not supposed to give a shit about women.

Perhaps fucking her was a bad idea because it sure as hell didn't get her off my brain. It did the complete fucking opposite. Now I can't think of anything else, and it's driving me insane.

The only logical thing I could do was drink—drink to forget.

"Alexander?" Margo's voice on the other side of the bedroom door pulls me away from my thoughts. "Are you nearly ready to leave for dinner?"

Fuck. I was out longer than I thought, but I'm still drunk. There's no way I'll be able to make it.

"I'm not going," I mutter loud enough for her to hear.

"But, you have to go. Yamada—"

"Will get over it," I finish for her. "Call him to cancel."

I roll onto my side and close my eyes, but the sound of my door flinging open and Margo's high heels clicking across the floor causes my eyes to snap open. "Margo? What are you—?"

Without permission, she leans over the bed, grabs my arm and yanks. "Come on. Get up. You can't cancel this meeting. I—"

Quickly I reach out and pull her down on the bed with me, causing her to shriek, not caring a bit if I wrinkle the bright-blue dress she's wearing. "You what? Need this meeting to try to get to know Yamada better?"

She squirms in my arms as she pushes against my chest. "Dammit, King, let me go. If you're not meeting with him, then I will."

"It's not going to work, Margo. You might as well stop trying. Yamada's *my* friend. He would never sell out on me. You're wasting your time."

She stops fighting for a split second and stares me in the eye. "I have to at least try. I have to at least go for what I want. Don't you understand that?"

Her words resonate with me so much. I've lived by the motto of getting what I want for years now. "More than you know."

She pushes me away and scrambles out of the bed. "I'm going. With or without you."

The clicking of her heels against the marble floor echoes around the room. I don't know where she thinks she's going, but she's not going to meet with my contact alone. No way in hell will I allow that to happen.

I'm up in a flash, crossing the room, and the second she grabs the door handle, I wrap my fingers around her wrist. "You're not going anywhere."

Her back tenses as I press my chest against it. The feel of the heat of her skin is almost more than I can take. I clutch her hip with my other hand and pull her ass against my cock. I want her to feel how hard I am to show her that I want her again.

Her head falls back slightly, sending her floral scent swarming around me, and there's a pant in her voice. "Don't tell me what to do."

I swipe her hair to the side, exposing her smooth flesh, and then whisper in her ear. "I'm your boss, baby. You'll do as I say."

I press my lips against the soft skin under her ear before I playfully nip it, needing desperately for her to give in to me.

The tension in her body loosens as she leans into me. "Damn you. We can't . . . You said—"

I grin, knowing that she's about to fold. She's flustered and I'm about to work that to my advantage and not give her a chance to pull herself together and refuse me.

"Fuck what I said before." I can no longer resist the urge to taste her. My tongue darts out and I trail a line down from below her ear down to her shoulder. "I need to fuck you. I can't get the thought of how good your pussy felt wrapped around my cock out of my head."

I knead her tit through her blouse, and she whimpers. "I hate what you do to me."

"No, you don't." I spin her around to face me and then cage her against the wall with my body. "You love it. You crave this just as much as I do, but you won't allow yourself to admit it."

Her breathing picks up speed and her chest heaves. "No."

"No?" I raise an eyebrow as I lean in and lick her top lip, causing her to shudder. "If you really meant that, then you wouldn't react so much when I touch you."

"You're such an egotistical asshole," she murmurs, but I can tell it's just her defense mechanism in full effect trying to fucking fight me tooth and nail.

"Come on, Margo." I reach down, grabbing behind her right knee, and hitch it around my hip. "I'm damn good at everything I do. Besides, being cocky is part of my charm. You know I'm the best lay you've ever had."

My heart thunders in my chest. She fits against me perfectly. I slide my hands down her back and rest them on her hips, where they rest so comfortably it's like they were made for my hands to hold on to. I have to have her again—experience the feeling of euphoria one more time.

My cock is rock hard in my shorts and it's driving me out of my mind knowing that only two thin pieces of fabric are holding me back from fucking Margo's brains out right here against this door. I grind myself against her and her mouth drops open.

I reach between us and stroke her clit through the silk panties she's wearing. "Mmm. So wet. This makes my mouth fucking water."

"What are you doing to me?" She moans. "I'm usually in control."

"That's what makes this exciting—letting go. No matter how much you try to fight it, you want me inside you just as much as I want to be there. Look at how your body reacts." I apply more pressure as I continue my slow teasing circles that won't bring her anywhere near climax. Her head falls back and bumps against the door as her fingers grip my biceps so tight I'm sure her nails will leave imprints.

"Alexander . . ." There's a plea in her voice. "We shouldn't. This is wrong."

I lean in so close that I can feel the warmth of her breath on my face. "Nothing about pleasure is wrong, Margo. I know that you hate me, but say yes to this. I need to have you at least one more time and then, I swear, I'll never ask again."

She bites her bottom lip as she debates my request while I continue to work my thumb against her. She won't be able to say no to this—say no to me.

Margo moans and then licks her lips. "This changes nothing between us. We are still enemies, and I plan to find a way to get my father's company back from you."

A grin spreads across my face as I realize that I've won. "I'd be disappointed if you didn't try."

My eyes drift down to her pouty lips and then back up to refocus on her gaze. There's hesitation in her eyes mixed with a hint of lust.

My fingertips find their way to her face, where they trace the smooth skin along her jaw. My cock throbs in anticipation. This woman seems to have that effect on me. "Margo—"

"Just shut up and kiss me before I change my mind," she whispers.

She doesn't have to tell me twice. I crush my lips into hers and my hands frantically begin to unzip her dress.

We shouldn't be doing this. We both know it. This . . . it's not good for business, but I just can't seem to fucking help myself. I've never wanted a woman so much that I was willing to throw all the fucking rules out the window just to have her. It's like none of it matters—everything I've worked for—when I'm around her. She drives me out of my mind with that smart mouth of hers—the way she stands up to me and tells me exactly what's on her mind. She's upfront—that's a trait to be admired because it's rarely seen anymore.

"Fuck. I want you," I tell her before I shove the dress off her shoulders and it falls in a pool around her feet. I deepen our kiss, loving the delicious taste. "So fucking bad it hurts."

My hungry eyes trail over every inch of her body. The black bra and matching satin panties are almost more than I can handle. I need them off.

Now.

When I unhook her bra, her puckered nipples rub against my solid chest. It makes me even more eager now that she's pressed against me. I don't think I can take my time with her. I want her too much. Without permission, I rip the thin fabric and toss it to the floor before I go back to attacking her lips. I fully expect Margo to yell at me for destroying yet another pair of her underwear, but she doesn't. She's just as caught up in this kiss as I am and only responds by shoving my shorts down. My cock springs free and it presses against her bare flesh. Margo throws her hands into my hair and holds me in place as our tongues tangle together.

I knew she wanted this just as much as I do.

Margo whimpers as my finger finds her swollen clit again for a moment before it glides inside her. "Mmm, you're so turned on. Feeling just how ready you are makes me want to fuck you hard and fast."

She groans as I work my finger in and out of her. "Alexander . . ."

I love hearing my name spill from her lips. It's nearly enough to cause me to blow my load on the spot. I can't believe how fucking turned on I am from just knowing that I'm making her body feel so good.

Margo claws at my back as I work her into a frenzy. The only thing better than this will be when my cock replaces my finger and I pound her into submission. "Your pussy is so fucking greedy. Do you feel how it's milking my finger, begging for my cock?" My tongue darts out to taste her lips. "You're so ready for me. Do you want me to take you? Right here? Right Now?"

"Yes," she pants.

The way she's panting causes my balls to tighten. I like hearing her practically beg me for it because it means she's losing control just like I am. Uptight Margo would never beg me for anything, but horny Margo seems much more open to bending to my will.

I trail my nose against her jaw, inhaling the scent of her before I whisper in her ear, "If you want my cock inside you, ask me for it. Ask me to fuck you. I need to hear you say it."

My thumb rubs circles over her swollen clit and her head falls back, bumping against the door. "Oh, so close."

"Say it," I command. "Ask me, and I'll make you feel so fucking good."

"Fuck me, Alexander," Margo says in a breathy voice.

I nibble on her bottom lip. "Good girl."

I hoist her up against the wall, unable to stop myself and press my bare shaft against her wet pussy. "I can't wait another fucking second."

My own breath catches the moment my bare cock glides into her warmth, allowing it to wrap around me. Her pussy squeezes every inch of my cock as I push in balls deep.

"Holy fuck," I say against her mouth. "You feel so fucking good."

I pull back slowly and then fill her again, giving her time to adjust to me. Margo whimpers against my lips, and I push into her one more time. The little noises she's making combined with how good she feels, are deadly. I won't be able to last. This time when I pull out of her I slam back in.

"Jesus!" Margo cries out. "Yes!"

Her cry only excites me more as I begin slamming into her. "Mmm, Margo. You like it hard, don't you? I knew you were a dirty girl."

I fuck her hard and fast against the door while she continues to claw at my back and scream out with delight. It feels so fucking good, and it doesn't take long for my balls to tighten.

"Oh, Alexander. Oh, God. I'm coming. Don't stop! Don't stop!" Margo cries out as she comes hard around my cock.

Watching her fall apart sends me over the edge and I pull out just in time to drop her legs to the ground and come all over her thighs. I pant hard as I lean my head against the wall over her right shoulder to catch my breath.

What in the holy fuck am I doing? I never fuck a woman more than once, and I for damn sure don't risk fucking one that could cost me billions of dollars. Why am I allowing this girl to get to me and fuck with my head? It's like I'm a fucking crack addict and she's the best hit I've ever had. I can't get enough, no matter what the cost.

I need to tell her to get the fuck out of this room and fire her ass. It's the only way I'll be able to make sure I don't slip up again.

I pull back and open my mouth, fully ready to turn back into a huge asshole, but the sight of Margo's bright-blue eyes narrowed at me causes me to snap it shut. I wasn't expecting that expression, considering I'd just given her one damn fine orgasm.

"You are such a bastard," she snaps.

I raise my eyebrows and pull back a bit. "Most women thank me for what I just did for you."

"Thank you?" She shakes her head and releases a bitter laugh. "Alexander, I should punch you in the face for ruining my Versace dress."

My gaze drops down to the floor, and I see her dress still in a pool by our feet only now it has my come on it from when I pulled out of her.

I smirk, unable to stop myself from finding a little humor in the situation. "Great sex requires sacrifice, and I'm afraid your dress paid the ultimate price."

"Ugh!" She growls as she shoves my shoulders back and steps away from me. "You're unbelievable." She bends over and snatches the dress off the floor. "From now on, stay the hell away from me. This will not be happening again."

I stare her down, meeting the challenge in her eyes. "Margo, don't kid yourself. If I want you again, all I have to do is touch you and you'll give in. Your body has already proven twice that it can't resist me."

She pulls her lips into a tight line. "Never. Again. Alexander, do you hear me? This—whatever it was—is over. Done. When we get back to New York, I'm going to figure out a way to bury you. You can count on it."

I give her my most wicked smile, showing her that her threats mean nothing to me. "I look forward to your sweet ass attempting to destroy me."

Her nostrils flare and I can tell she wants nothing more than to lay into me. Instead, she takes a deep breath, squares her shoulders, and flips me the middle finger.

I laugh and then chide, "Mature."

Margo jerks open the door while she's still bare ass naked. "Fuck you."

"I thought you just said we weren't doing that again?" I tease.

"You . . . I . . . Ugh!" That's all she manages to get out before storming out in nothing but her stilettos and slamming the door behind her.

I drop my head into my hand and then run it over the top of my head. What the actual fuck just happened? That spiraled out of control quickly and I didn't even have to say a damn word. I guess I don't have to ask her to stay away from me, after all.

The sharp ring of my cell cuts across the otherwise quiet room, not giving me the time to think about what in the hell just happened. I pull my shorts back up before walking over to the nightstand and smiling as I see the name of the caller flash across the screen.

"King," I answer.

"Where are you, asshole? Yamada's been waiting on you all night. First you blow off dinner and now drinks at the bar?" There's irritation in his voice.

"Look, man, I'm sorry. I had too much to drink today so I'm staying in for the night, but I promise tomorrow we'll party."

I know that I flew out here to spend the weekend with him and secure the deal with our companies for the Buchanan deal but going out to find random women to party with doesn't sound appealing.

"Okay. Fine. But, I'm holding you to tomorrow. You better bring your 'A' game because it's going to be Yamada and King just like the old days. Getting' bitches and gettin' laid."

I chuckle. "You got it, buddy. Tomorrow, Vegas better watch out."

"Make sure you bring Dime Piece back with you. She's got a rockin' body, and I wouldn't mind—"

"Goodnight, Yamada."

I quickly cut him off before he has a chance to finish whatever dirty thought was brewing in that twisted little mind of his. Besides, it pisses me off for some reason when he talks about how sexy Margo is. I know he's harmless, and I can't believe I'm admitting this, but the idea of another man looking at Margo makes me jealous as hell.

This is going to be a fucking problem.

Chapter XII
HOLY SHIT

Margo

Stupid. Stupid. Stupid. That's the word I've been scolding myself with since last night. I can't believe that I had sex with Alexander King . . . *again.* Even after I forbid myself from ever doing it again, the moment he put his hands on me in his room I was a goner.

I hate that the man has so much power over my body.

When he texted me early this morning to demand my presence in the common area of our suite for breakfast, I replied with a friendly fuck off. Not the most mature thing to do, I know. Normally, I play it cooler when dealing with assholes like Alexander, but for some strange reason, he's able to get under my skin like no one else and cause me to lose my typical level head.

I spent most of the day in my room with the door locked trying to figure out ways I could avoid Alexander while still maintaining a close presence to figure out a way to get between him and Yamada. From what little bit of background I know about their relationship, it seems that they go way back, but hopefully their bond has a weak point I can break into.

The hotel phone rings, pulling my attention away from my thoughts and I answer on the third ring. "Hello?"

"Dime Piece! Are you coming to my party tonight?" Yamada's upbeat voice laced with his heavy accent shoots across the line.

I lift my eyebrows. "Alexander didn't mention anything."

"King said you hate him right now and wouldn't come even if he asked, but I knew if Yamada invited you up to his penthouse, you couldn't turn that down."

I roll my eyes and laugh to myself. Yamada really is convinced that he's quite the ladies' man.

Yamada's also wrong about Alexander. Alexander didn't tell me about the party because he knew I would jump at the chance to spend a little one-on-one time to pick Yamada's brain. Alexander kept this from me on purpose. He knows how badly I want to talk with Yamada. Alexander wants to limit my access to the man who whill have a huge hand in the destruction of my father's company.

King has another thing coming if he thinks he can keep me from my main objective while we're here.

"So, are you coming or not?" Yamada asks.

I lift my chin. "I'm in. What time does it start?"

"It's already in full swing, so get your smokin' self up here. I'm in the Real World suite. I'll send my security down in thirty minutes to escort you up."

"I'll be ready," I tell him.

"Great. See you then, you sexy thing." I hear the smile in his voice, and I can't help shaking my head.

Out of every type of business partner I imagined Alexander King to have, Yamada was definitely unexpected.

When I pass through what I have officially dubbed 'The Room That Shall Not Be Named' on the way to the common area of the suite, I shudder the moment my eyes land on the table. The things that man did to my body on there are unspeakable in the best kinds of ways. It's hard to admit the man that you love to hate can make you feel so incredibly good.

A quick rap on the door makes me quicken my pace. I open the door and find two very large official looking men in black suits—one white guy with short buzzed blond hair and the other a light-skinned black man with braids—each of them at least six-foot-five or better because they dwarf me by at least a foot.

The man with braids gives me a polite smile. "Good evening, miss. We're here to escort you to Mr. Yamada's suite."

I nod stepping out into the hallway with them and closing the door behind me. The ride up in the elevator to Yamada's penthouse is quick, but I find myself fidgeting with the hem of my black dress, trying to squeeze an extra inch from the length to cover more thigh. This is the shortest one I brought, and suddenly, I wish I wouldn't have picked this one to wear to a place I know Alexander will be in attendance. I don't need the temptation of having him come on to me. Lord knows that I can't seem to resist his advances, so I need to make sure I steer clear and don't set myself up for another encounter with him.

When the elevator dings and the doors open, the men lead me down the hallway. They pause at a set of double doors and use their keycard to gain entrance into Yamada's suite. It doesn't surprise me that this suite is the biggest one in the hotel.

Wall to wall bodies fill the large space as music pumps through the air. People are dancing to the beat while sipping on drinks like the place is one of Vegas' hottest nightclubs. I follow the security team closely as we wind our way through the crowd. Yamada seems very eccentric and over-the-top, so this place totally fits him.

The crashing sound of bowling pins smashing into one another catches my attention, and I raise my eyebrows when I find a full-fledged bowling lane in the suite just a little ways down from the hot tub that's filled with bikini-clad women.

Turning the corner, I see a large white sectional crammed with people. My heart freezes in my chest the moment my eyes land on Alexander, who has two women strategically placed on either side of him. He hasn't spotted me just yet because I follow his line of sight and his gaze is fixed on Yamada, who is standing in front of him wearing a flat bill baseball cap turned sideways, low-riding jeans, and a white buttoned-down dress shirt that's undone to reveal a T-shirt underneath. Yamada seems to be telling a story of some sort because he's throwing his hands around causing Alexander to laugh. I stop in my tracks and just stare. It's the first time I've ever actually seen Alexander look relaxed and happy, and it's breathtaking. The casual outfit he has on of jeans and a T-shirt looks amazing. He's never looked more handsome, and from the outside looking in, he looks like a carefree spirit—one I wish I knew instead of the asshole I fucked . . . twice.

"Sir, Ms. Buchanan, as requested," the blond security guy says, interrupting Yamada's joke.

Alexander's eyes immediately snap in my direction, and the jovial expression that I was just admiring has completely been wiped off his face. His posture even changes and instead of leaning forward toward his friend, he relaxes back against the couch and throws his arms around the women on either side of him, pulling them snug against his sides.

My nostrils flare. That asshole. What's he trying to do—make me jealous? Ha! Well, I'll show him that it doesn't bother me one tiny bit.

I'm here for one reason: To get close to Yamada. I will not allow Alexander King to distract me no matter how ridiculous he looks draped over some random bottle-blondes.

Yamada turns to me and holds out his arms. "Dime Piece! I knew you wouldn't refuse Yamada! Come give Papa some love."

I hold back a laugh and an eye roll as I step into his embrace and hug the guy back. "This party is really something. Do you know all these people?"

Yamada pulls back and then places his hands on his hips as he surveys the filled space. "No, but the bitch—"

"Bitches love Yamada," Alexander cuts him off. "I'm sure you've told her that one already."

I curl my lip at Alexander. "He can tell me again if he wants. You shouldn't be a complete asshole and cut people off like that. It's rude, and you've got a bad habit of doing it."

Alexander's eyes narrow at me. He hates when I belittle him. This grumpy look he's giving me is the same one I get every time I tell him something he doesn't want to hear.

Yamada bursts out in a fit of laughter. “Yamada’s in love. Any woman who stands up to King earns my respect.” He grabs my arm. “Come on. Let’s go get you a drink.”

He pulls me through the crowd to where he has two bartenders working what appears to be a full bar. “What are you drinking?”

I bite my lower lip. “I don’t typically drink, so just a diet soda or water would be fine.”

Yamada tilts his head and stares at me like I’ve just sprouted wings. “What? Are you one of those Christian-y types or something?”

I shake my head. “No. I just like to keep my head on straight. People always seem to do crazy things when they drink.”

The corner of Yamada’s mouth lifts into a half smile. “That’s kind of the point—to let loose and have some fun.”

His words ring through my head and I think back on the phone conversation I had with my mother just before I boarded the plane. I did promise her that I would have at least one drink and not be a complete stiff while I was out here. What’s the worst that can happen?

I push up to the bar and the cute dark-haired bartender looks my way with a smile on his face. “What can I get you?”

“Can I get a screwdriver?” I ask and the guy nods and gets to work making my order.

Yamada’s smile widens. “That’s the spirit.” He turns toward the bartender. “Make that two. We’re getting fucked up tonight!”

Three drinks later, Yamada and I are dancing to some crazy techno sounding song that I’ve never heard, but with all the alcohol coursing through my veins, I’m not bothered that I might look like an idiot.

Yamada sings along—complete with doing the rap to the song that completely comes out of nowhere. He flings his hands and points his fingers while spitting out the fast-paced words just like the guys do on the videos.

"You're pretty good at that," I lean in to tell him. "You should be a rapper or something."

He smiles. "That's exactly what Yamada's going to be, waiting for his one shot to be discovered."

"Why don't you make your own video and put it on YouTube or something? You have the money."

He nods. "Yamada might just do that while he's here in the states. Good thinkin,' Dime Piece. Beautiful and smart. No wonder you have King tripping all over himself."

I roll my eyes before I nod my head in the direction of the couch where we left Alexander sitting with the two women. "Clearly, he's not. He couldn't care less about me."

He puts his hand on my shoulder. "Don't let that show over there fool you. Trust me. The Barbie Twins are a cover—for his own benefit—to make you think that he's not thinking about you,when, in fact, he is. He just isn't ready to admit it to you or himself yet that he cares."

"You can't possibly know that."

"But I do," he assures me. "He warned me that you were off-limits."

I shake my head. "That's only because of my father. Alexander's afraid that I'm here to try to mess up the deal the two of you have going for parts of my Buchanan Industries."

"That's not it. Trust me. Alexander knows that nothing you could do would pull my loyalty away from him."

That hurts, knowing there's nothing I can do to make Yamada change his mind about my father's company. I guess it's time to face the facts. Alexander has won this war. It's not fair and it's wrong in so many ways, but there doesn't seem to be anything I can do to stop Yamada's company from making a deal with Alexander.

I sigh and drop my head. "I'm such an idiot. I'm a project to him—nothing more—and I'm stupid for letting him in my pants. I'm usually a lot smarter and don't allow myself to lose control. He said he was going to torture me until I quit. I guess fucking me and then showing me that I mean nothing to him is his tactic to get me to do that."

Yamada tips my chin back up with his bent index finger. "Don't discount yourself like that. The last girl King warned Yamada to stay away from was Jess, and he was madly in love with her. The guy turned into a jealous maniac whenever another man even thought about breathing in her direction. I haven't seen him act that way—all possessive and shit—toward another woman since then—not until this weekend with you, that is."

I furrow my brow. "What are you saying?"

Yamada sighs, and his eyes soften a bit. "He's different with you. King can be an asshole—everyone knows that—but you have to be able to see past all that to see the real him."

I glance over at Alexander, who is watching Yamada and me intently. His words about seeing the real Alexander waft through my head as I remember how happy Alexander looked when I first spotted him tonight. Is it possible for me to even get to know that guy? Would he ever be like that with me?

The short answer to that is no. It's never going to happen. Alexander sees me as the enemy and nothing is ever going to change that. For some reason knowing that fact causes my stomach to twist.

I take a deep breath. Being in this room while I break down can't happen. I won't allow Alexander King to see me cry. That implies weakness and I need to maintain a strong front when it comes to him.

"I'll be back," I tell Yamada before I take off in search of a restroom.

My eyes burn and I have no idea why in the hell I'm allowing the situation with Alexander to get to me at this very moment.

Must be the damn liquor that's flowing through my veins. It's causing my emotions to surface at the most inopportune time.

When I finally find the bathroom, I rush through the door and place my hands on the counter. I close my eyes as I count down from ten to calm myself. Mother taught me as a little girl to do this when I felt my emotions getting out of check. It has always helped me to regain control and refocus on the situation with a level head.

"Three . . . Two . . . One . . ." I count aloud but the sound of the bathroom door opening causes my eyes to snap open. "Someone is in here."

"I know that." Alexander's deep voice cuts through the room as he closes the door and locks it, closing us in the tiny space together. "Are you okay?"

"I'm fine." I sigh as I stare at him through the mirror when he walks up behind me. "What are you doing in here?"

He raises one eyebrow. "Is it wrong that I came in to check on you? You've had a lot to drink. I wanted to make sure you weren't in here puking your guts out."

I turn to face him and fold my arms over my chest. "So what if I was. It's not like you care."

He flinches. "Do you really think that I'm that big of an asshole that I wouldn't come to check on you? While we're out here, you're my responsibility to keep safe."

"No. I'm not. I can take care of myself," I fire back.

"I'm aware that you're fully capable of handling yourself, but that doesn't mean that I don't . . ."

"Don't what?" I prod.

"Care, all right? I'd care if you were all alone in here sick. " He pinches the bridge of his nose and shuts his eyes for a brief second. "I'm not a dick all of the time."

"Just most of the time, then?" His omission causes me to smile. Maybe I need to give Yamada some credit. He might not be so far off the mark, after all.

Alexander shakes his head as he closes the distance between us and backs me up against the counter. He drags his teeth slowly over his bottom lip as he reaches up and cups my face. "Why can't I leave you alone?"

The question seems more rhetorical than directed at me, but I'm curious as well.

"Why didn't you come to breakfast this morning?" he asks as he stares into my eyes.

"I couldn't bear the thought of seeing you after last night. I was angry at myself for letting things go that far with you . . . again, after I promised myself that it wouldn't," I admit.

He nods like he fully understands where I'm coming from. "We really do need to try to stay away from each other."

I let out a shaky breath and try to pretend that being so close to him, feeling the warmth of his breath on my face isn't sending my body into overdrive. "Any idea how to make sure that happens?"

"Touching is a bad idea. It leads me to think about that sweet pussy of yours. And how good it feels when I'm inside you. We should avoid doing that if we don't want to end up fucking again, but that might be complicated." He traces my jaw with his thumb. "I've tasted your sweetness, and I know what I'd be missing out on by denying myself, and I never tell myself no if it's something that I really want."

I swallow hard as his gray eyes remain locked on me. "What are you saying?"

"I'm saying since I'm sure by now that you know there's no swaying Yamada away from me with whatever plan you came out here with, we might as well enjoy the rest of the weekend . . . and each other."

My brows furrow. "You want me to be your fuck buddy for the weekend?"

His shoulders rise in a noncommittal shrug. "If you must put a label on it, then yes. I want you to willingly give yourself to me for the weekend, whenever I want to fuck."

"No," I instantly respond and push him back a bit so that there's more space between us. Having him so close clouds my judgment. "I told you before we came out here to not expect me to be one of your paid whores. I don't work like that."

"Who said anything about paying you? You've fucked me twice already for free."

My nostrils flare as I pull back and smack him with all my might. "You're such a bastard."

The spot on his cheek where I made contact turns scarlet, and he raises his hand to rub the spot. "So that's a no then?"

I flip him off. "That's a hell fucking no."

I don't give him another minute to say anything else before I storm out of the bathroom. The party is still in full swing, but I don't feel like having fun anymore. I'm mad as hell. It's one thing to make a mistake by sleeping together, but it's an entirely different thing when he insinuates that I'm an easy slut.

That bastard will never get into these panties again.

Yamada stands in front me, blocking my path as I head toward the door. "Whoa there. Where are you running off to?"

"I'm going back to my room."

"Why?" Yamada asks. "King pissed you off, huh?"

"He's an asshole." It's all I can manage to say.

Yamada smiles. "He is, but you already knew that. He's testing you."

I flinch. "Testing me? For what?"

He shrugs. "To see how much of his bullshit you will put up with before you leave him. He's trying to push you away so that he doesn't have to open up to you. It's a defense mechanism. Every woman he's opened up to has left him." I stare at Yamada with my mouth agape, which only causes his smile to widen. "Come on, Dime Piece. Don't look so shocked. Yamada is not only devastatingly handsome with an amazing personality, but he's an intelligent madafucka too with a minor in psychology."

I stand there flabbergasted. "So you're saying that I should stay?"

"Yes," he answers. "Show him that he doesn't intimidate you, and that you'll stand your ground."

I sigh deeply. He's probably right. It's not like I'll never have to see Alexander again after we leave Vegas. I'm still his employee. I'll need to stand my ground and prepare myself for when I see him at work so that he knows that I'm not someone he can shove around and bend to his will.

"Okay, but I think I'm going to need another drink," I say.

"That's the spirit," Yamada praises before grabbing my hand and towing me back through the crowd. "I've got to take a leak. Go get that drink."

As soon as Yamada walks off, I step up to the bar and order a shot of tequila, needing to drink myself into oblivion if I'm going to coexist in the same room with Alexander.

I sense him before I feel him, and there's no question who has just flanked my side. Alexander's chest pushes against my arm. His spicy cologne fills my nose and my mouth waters.

Gah! Stop it! Even his damn scent is sexy.

"I'm surprised to find you still here," Alexander growls into my ear. "I figured you'd be holed up in your room down in our sex den."

I turn and level my stare with his. His eyes hold so many questions—ones I'm sure he's waiting for me to answer—but I'm not going to give him what he wants. Instead I decide to do a little teasing of my own. "Yamada's argument for me to stay was *very* compelling."

He obviously wasn't expecting that response because he raises both of his eyebrows and he licks his lips nervously. "And what, might I ask, did he say to you?"

I shrug. "That's between Yamada and me. We're really bonding, you know. I'm sure it won't be long now before he considers me a friend too and cuts my father a deal instead of you."

Instead of getting mad like I expect, Alexander chuckles. I grip the counter a little tighter than needed be to keep myself from smacking his condescending face yet again.

"Margo, I really wish you would stop trying to outdo me in everything. You'll eventually learn that I always win. It's silly for you to keep expelling energy on any other outcome. I get my way in all things."

I roll my eyes. "That's not possible. Everyone loses at some point or another."

Alexander smiles. "Not me."

"Well, neither do I," I say just as the bartender sets my shot down. I instantly pick it up and throw it back.

"Whoa. You might want to slow down there, lightweight, or you really will be throwing up later."

I scowl at him. "Don't tell me what to do. Besides, I can probably hold my liquor better than you can.

He smiles. "Is that so?"

I give him a curt nod. "Absolutely."

Okay, so maybe I was exaggerating a bit here, but I refuse to let him get the best of me.

"Well, you'll just have to prove that to me then." Alexander holds up five fingers to the bartender and then points down to my empty glass before looking back at me. "To make it fair since I'm quite a bit bigger than you, I'll drink two shots for every one of yours."

The bartender sets five tequila-filled shots in front of us, and Alexander does two of them immediately and then flips the glasses upside down on the counter before pushing another shot over to me. "Now we're even. Ready to prove me right? First one to puke, loses."

"You're on." I pick up one of the shots and tip it back with ease. "Hope you're prepared for that pride of yours to get crushed when I kick your overconfident ass."

Alexander takes the other two shots, but his eyes stay trained on me the entire time. "And just so you know, I'm not one of those romantic bastards who will hold back your hair when you're praying to the porcelain god."

I wrinkle my nose at him. "I don't plan on doing that anytime soon."

The sound of bowling pins falling catches Alexander's attention and his eyes light up. "Come on. Let me kick your ass at bowling too."

After three games of bowling, I find myself genuinely having a good time hanging out with Alexander. The more we drank, the more fun I had, even though I'll never admit that to him. He's actually pretty entertaining when he drops the world's biggest prick act.

"We need more drinks," Alexander announces after he bowls the last ball, winning his second game out of the three we played. "I believe I just won our little competition. I'll be back. Let me know if you want me to kick your ass again when I get back."

I laugh, staring after him as he walks away to get more drinks. His ass in the dark-washed jeans he's wearing looks amazing.

I plop down in the chair as I wait on Alexander to bring the drinks, and Yamada appears in front of me. "Looks like someone's having fun now."

I shake my head and attempt to scowl, but a smile keeps popping up. "No. I'm having zero fun."

Yamada's expression is one of disbelief as he sits down next to me. "Then what was all the laughing Yamada heard over here?"

"Oh, that." I wave him off dismissively. "That was just Alexander wiggling his ass a little before he took every shot to distract me. It was so ridiculous that I couldn't help laughing."

"Shot number seven for the lady and thirteen and fourteen for me," Alexander says as he approaches Yamada and me with three shots.

Everything around me is a little cloudy and I know all the liquor is messing with me big time, but I'm doing my best to pretend that it's not.

"The two of you are going to regret this tomorrow," Yamada says in sympathy as Alexander and I clink our glasses together and down the liquid. "Everyone's leaving and Yamada is ready to go out on the town. Let's find another place to party and find trouble."

"I'm game," Alexander says as he extends his hand to me.

"Why not," I answer taking his hand and allowing him to help me up.

The moment I'm on my feet, Alexander wraps his strong arms around me and buries his face in my hair, inhaling deeply. "You smell so fucking good. Are you sure you want to go out? We could just go back to our suite . . ."

Heat instantly pulses through me while my body craves nothing more than to go to our room to go crazy on each other. But even in my drunken state, I know that's a bad idea.

I press my hand against his chest. "No. We're going out."

Alexander sighs and presses his lips to the sensitive flesh just below my ear. "If that's what you want. But—" he pulls away, but reaches down and threads his large fingers through mine and grins "—I'm not letting go of you tonight. No other man is going to have you if I can't."

My heart does a double thump against my ribcage as Alexander leads me out of the penthouse behind Yamada. That might be the nicest and most romantic thing anyone's ever said to me. Who knew Alexander King was capable of that?

The sound of the maids running the vacuum somewhere in the hallway wakes me and my head instantly begins to throb. Thank God for heavy hotel curtains that block out the sun, but I still don't dare open up my eyes.

The bed I'm in bounces a little and I instantly freeze. I pull in a deep breath through my nose to steady myself and peel open one eye to spot a shirtless Alexander King sprawled out next to me.

I grimace and cover my face with my hands.

Oh. My. God. How could I let this happen?

I continue to mentally scold myself as I try to remember exactly what happened last night, but everything is such a blur. The last thing I remember was Alexander winning at bowling and him whispering possessively in my ear that made my knees a little weak and then leaving to go to a club. That's it.

Hopefully, we just fell asleep in the same bed together. I lift the covers and stare down at my completely naked body. I'm guessing we had some hot, sweaty sex again. But I was too drunk to remember it and too drunk to force my body to listen to my head and not give in and fuck this man again.

Shit.

I grab the blanket with my left hand to pull it back so I can slip out of this bed before he wakes up. A single ray of sunlight cuts through the small opening in the curtain and shines on my hand, causing a brilliant sparkle to catch my attention.

I stare down at my hand and my mouth falls open as I spot a diamond wedding band on my ring finger.

"Holy shit!" I yell.

What in the holy hell is going on? My eyes focus on the ring as I desperately try to remember how this got on my finger last night because it's definitely not a gag ring judging by the size of this thing. It's a fucking monster and looks pretty real to me.

Alexander rolls over and rubs his face while he asks in a groggy voice, "What the fuck?"

My eyes practically bulge out of their sockets when I notice Alexander's left hand has a ring on it too. I grab his hand and yank it closer to my face to inspect it. The sound of screams echo around the room, and it takes a second for me to register that it's me who's doing it.

"Ah. Shit, Margo. My ears," Alexander complains.

"Look at this!" I order as I hold his hand up in front of his face so his eyes can focus on the ring on his own hand.

Alexander immediately sits up straight as a board in bed, suddenly wide awake, and his face contorts in disbelief. "What the . . . how . . . YAMADA?!"

The sound of bare feet slapping against the tile floor comes barreling towards us. When the bedroom door flies open, Yamada stands there wearing nothing but a pair of tighty-whities underwear and a black silk robe and a huge smile. "Happy honeymoon, madafakas!"

END PART ONE

Feisty Princess (A Sexy Manhattan Fairytale Part II)

Coming Soon

About the Author

New York Times and USA Today Best Selling author Michelle A. Valentine is a Central Ohio nurse turned author of erotic and New Adult romance of novels. Her love of hard-rock music, tattoos and sexy musicians inspires her naughty novels.

Find her:
Website (http://www.michelleavalentine.com) | Facebook (http://www.facebook.com/AuthorMichelleAValentine) |
Twitter (https://twitter.com/M_A_Valentine)
Blog Site (http://michelleavalentine.blogspot.com/) |
Subscribe to my Newsletter
(https://www.facebook.com/AuthorMichelleAValentine/app_100265896690345) | Email Me
(mailto:michellevalentineauthor@gmail.com)